THE
HAUNTED

RENE M GERRITS

Tellwell Talent
www.tellwell.ca

ISBN
978-0-2288-5412-8 (Hardcover)
978-0-2288-5411-1 (Paperback)
978-0-2288-5413-5 (eBook)

To Michelle, who was always eager
to read every draft of this book and affectionately
Calls it, "Her Novel." Love you.

CONTENTS

CHAPTER ONE

THE INTRIGUE

Sitting in his office, sifting through a plethora of paperwork or what he deemed way too much, Will sat back in his tall leather chair, a sigh of disappointment heaving his chest.

His hazel eyes turned their attention to a glass of scotch on the far corner of his desk. He instinctively reached for it as he continued to read the document. With the synopses of his day and the results of his latest venture, it seemed the only thing he could rely on anymore for some form of immediate satisfaction was a hard drink.

Another haunt busted, he thought to himself as he sipped the peaty nectar. After putting the glass down on the ring of condensation it had previously left, he began to look through the paperwork once more just to be certain. Electronic Voice Recordings (EVR) were non-existent, though the homeowners reported that on many occasions, they'd heard phantom footsteps marching up and down the stairs at night. He put the papers back into the file folder and removed the photographs. Black-and-white infrared photos yielded results, but they were all explanatory. Vents and other devices that produced heat or different temperatures were at fault for the vivid photographs that, to the untrained person, would seem to be a gaseous entity. Even the Electro Magnetic Field Meter (EMF) readings were standard throughout the house. But he acknowledged that four days in a "haunted" house is not sufficient time to do thorough research. He felt somewhat bad that he was mailing off results arguably wrong in the eyes of the homeowners who believed so fervently their abode was infested with the spirits of the husband and wife that lived there for the duration of their lives. She had passed away in her sleep; he'd suffered a heart attack in his den watching *Murder She Wrote*.

Will gave it four days before he would hear back from the couple who believed the previous owners of their house refused to leave. It wouldn't be the first time he'd been slandered by some disgruntled client because he was unable to produce results that would fortify their claims of some paranormal phenomenon on their property. Some people just accepted the results and moved on, either to another investigator who would tell them what they wanted to hear, or they'd simply try to rationalize it from other angles.

A voice behind him made him jump. "Are you done with the case files? We're sending out the last of the reports and would like to include your findings from the case."

Will turned to meet Richard, whose six-foot-four frame towered in the doorway. He dwarfed Will at his five foot ten inches and was much leaner. They both were avid gym-goers, but Richard always seemed to look fit. Richard was always smiling. His eyes were happy. He was Will's adopted brother, and they looked nothing alike as Richard was adopted from South Africa when he was just a young child after Will's parents couldn't have any more children. Will had known there were many complications during the pregnancy, and he'd nearly died during childbirth. He never really understood it as a child, and with Richard, he didn't have to try. This made Richard a blessing in their eyes and Will's younger brother.

"Yes, I have it all here," Will muttered, unsatisfied as he compiled it once more into the folder and handed it to Richard, who accepted it with a smile.

"Thanks, Will," Richard said and then paused. "You know, you and I have seen many things and disproved a great deal of them. But we have been unable to establish neither reasonable nor earthly cause for so many more, but to account for paranormal influence or entities, that stands for something."

Will raised an eyebrow, wondering where his brother was going with this.

Richard's dark eyes glanced over to the glass of scotch on Will's desk, and he shook his head in disapproval as he set the folder down on the desk and opened the drawer. He removed the bottle and paused. "You are the best at parapsychology and paranormal research. I don't know what exactly it is that you are searching for, Will, but I'm positive you will find it."

At that, he raised the bottle as Will held up his glass, and the two had a drink to another "successful" paranormal investigation. Then Richard left the office with files in hand.

Will sat back, thinking for a moment. Rich was the one who originally was so intrigued by the unknown, and it was his passion that pulled Will into his world. He found that he had an uncanny ability for researching paranormal phenomena. He chuckled to himself, thinking of how Richard embraced and encouraged his development, and together they started their own research firm that dealt with cases all over the UK & North America. Sometimes they would travel abroad for a case that was of particular interest. He recalled the time he went to see a psychic after his uncle had passed away, not so much to try to communicate with the dead, even though he did miss his uncle, but he was doing personal research on psychics, dealing with his own scepticism until he met one who made him sit up in his chair.

"Who is Peter?" the psychic started, and he would never forget how astonished he was when she opened up with his late Uncle Peter. During the session, she directed him to his throat. "Do you ever have a hard time swallowing or get a mild irritation in your throat when you are on one of your expeditions?"

He looked at her inquisitively.

"It's because you have what is known as ectoplasm in you, right here." She directed him toward her jugular. "You have a gift, Mr. William. Work on developing it. That will be thirty dollars."

Will shook his head and shrugged the memory away as he left his chair to meet Stacey pushing her way through his door, which almost hit him as it swung open. She turned, immediately startled, as he plopped back into his chair from the near-miss.

"Oh my gosh! I am so sorry, Will! Are you alright?" she posed with concern while suppressing a giggle.

"Fine. What have you for me, Miss Stacey?" He eyed the folder she held to her chest while he regained his composure.

She marched over and gave him the file she had in her hand and stepped back, nervously tugging on her skirt and straightening the non-existent wrinkles out of it.

"I read a bit of the file, Mr. Will. It seems like your typical haunt." She paused. "But, I don't know, there seems like there is something more to it? Just...seems...different."

She caught his gaze and cleared her throat, regaining herself. "Richard will be helping you with the electrical equipment, but he will come a day after you arrive. He has another house to attend to first."

"Thank you, Miss Stacey," Will said with a smile.

"Be careful, Mr. Will," was all she said as she left the room. Stacey was, for the most part, quite bubbly and cheerful. Typically, she brightened any room she ventured into. Sometimes the atmosphere between her and Richard was a little overbearing. Neither one of them was married, and though they swore their relationship was strictly plutonic, one could easily assume they were lovers, and Will found it a little too much at times. Other investigative teams that may occasionally join them on a case would muse at the antics between Richard and Stacey—often taking bets to find out if, in fact, they were a couple.

He browsed through the file, curious of what he was up against. He also wanted to familiarize himself with the travel arrangements. He was to leave the following morning and would be met by the family butler to take him to a haunted estate in Brackenstone. He sifted through the pictures of the place pulled from books and other sources claiming it was haunted. His fingers grazed the photographs taken by the owner. He was impressed; it appeared to be built in the mid-to-late eighteen hundreds.

Spooky, he thought as he turned his attention to the details of the haunt. He raised his eyebrows. There was a lot of "activity" surrounding the house and the massive grounds it rested on. But what he found most intriguing was the personalized letter requesting his presence and expertise.

Stilton Paranormal Research Institute.
79 Black Dog Square
Canterbury, Kent.
South East England

Dearest Mr. William Stilton,

Your presence and talents are requested post haste at the Law Estate to put to rest the unsettled and superstitious. Should you accept this task, I shall look forward to seeing you at your earliest convenience.

Sincerely,

Mrs. Eleanor Law.

Law Estates
2814 Pilgrim Road
Brackenstone, Somerset.
South West England

He put the letter back into the folder and closed it up. After placing it in his carry bag, he exited his office.

Activity. He muddled over the very word. *It's all relative.* But he felt a rush of excitement. A new case was always exciting. No two haunts were the same. Though they may share similar characteristics of typical haunts, they were never the same. It was just what he needed, a new case on a large, eerie estate. Judging by the pictures, it was the kind of place one only reads about in books—a foreboding and forlorn place in appearance any paranormal expert would dream of going. A wave of enthusiasm surged through him. Perhaps he would discover new and exciting evidence that would explain the unexplainable world of the paranormal. He pushed his way through the door into the evening sunlight.

CHAPTER TWO

THE SCEPTIC

Richard, being his usual chipper self, was outside waiting in his car with two coffees posed in the van's coffee holders. He was excited about the case, but unlike Will, who hadn't said much in the office, he was very expressive about it. He took some time to pour over the Law estate files before Stacey had delivered them to his brother. Judging by the pictures, he knew Will wouldn't pass it up. He also knew he'd be driving there with all of their technical equipment once he was done with a consultation at an Inn known as the Barking Dane. Studying a map, he discovered that Brackenstone appeared to be an isolated town surrounded by agriculture and thousands of hectares of forest.

There was a *click* as the passenger door opened, and Will climbed into the van.

"You don't seem too thrilled about this new case, Will," he said with a hint of concern in his voice as his brother settled in the passenger seat.

Will grabbed the coffee, lifted the lid, and took a sip. It was strong enough to give a bison the shakes. "I am," he said in a mocking monotone voice. "I'm just not as expressive about it as you are." He paused. "And your morning chipper is putting a damper on my grogginess."

Richard chuckled to himself. "Not much sleep last night, I gather."

Will took another sip of his caffeinated brew. "I was looking at any online directories of the Law estate and researching the history of the estate itself. Turns out it is an orchard and a vineyard.

Richard nodded in approval, looking at Will. "You're not still sore over the last case, are you? I mean, we found lots of 'orbs' on the standard photographs, and we captured them on tape! That has to stand for something. Some say that orbs are angels."

Will stayed silent for a moment as if thinking. He sipped his coffee again. "This so good and so gross. Why do I find myself wanting to drink it, and yet, I have such a distaste for it? Ugh." He put it down in the tray before continuing, "Orbs are one of the most common forms of paranormal activity found. Everybody finds orbs, and they get so excited about it. Not to mention there are a variety of factors that disprove orbs as entities on SLR film or digital media."

Richard nodded again. "True. But not on video."

Will finished his coffee with one last heaping gulp. "Not on video," he said with a smile. "Besides, I can make angels with my ass." He laughed when Richard shot him an unapproving glance. Richard shared Will's enthusiasm for everything paranormal, and like his brother, he was a sceptic who believed that the more you cannot disprove something with hardened evidence, the more you are, in fact, proving it. But unlike Will, he wasn't so emotionally invested. He knew his brother had some kind of ethereal connection with the supernatural that neither one of them understood, and quite possibly both were too scared to try.

Will liked his little gadgets, such as his compass that would spin when introduced to an electromagnetic field or his infrared thermometer. He also prized his electronic voice recorder that would pick up audio the human ear could not hear, his electromagnetic field meter, and even his regular SLR camera. Richard was a techie and thrived off anything that he could connect to his laptops, such as CCTV cameras, infrared lenses, and motion sensor tech to capture video or still photographs. He could slow videos down or speed them up, play with their resolution, or cancel out background noise for clearer audio. They both knew that they were equally invested, with Richard being more the sceptic, but Will would never admit it.

Will slept for most of the three-hour plane ride after his layover in London, which made the journey closer to five hours. While sitting in the terminal, he took some time to review the files once again. He hoped to find something more, but there was little to go on. It was an area unknown to him. He had been to Somerset on many occasions, and he'd never heard of Brackenstone. Nor had he heard mention of it in the paranormal community or in books and journals regarding the topic. Nevertheless, he was glad to be the first, to his knowledge, to search out whatever "phenomena" it may possess. What he did manage to find out was that the current Law estate was a residence built in 1852 by a wealthy member of the British East India Trading Company who desired a more solitary life. Brackenstone, as it is now called, was originally a forestry community that harvested large timbers that would be floated down the waterway for miles to be used in ship building. But that was all the history he could find.

Will was slightly disappointed upon arrival when he noticed that instead of a butler waiting with a fancy automobile, there was a rented car. The driver, a bent, older chap, stood beside the right rear passenger door and waved him over. When Will inquired how the older man knew who he was, the gentleman merely stated that he looked lost, which was giveaway enough. It was a quiet ride to the Law estate just outside of Brackenstone. It was a quiet, drab town with a hazy atmosphere, like walking into a pub after its patrons had had a long night of drinking and merrymaking. The air was filled with odours and vapours from the surrounding forests and swamps. Old shops lined the streets, small boutiques, dining restaurants, and inns with pubs dotted here and there for the more mellow and rambunctious. Between the breaks of the buildings, Will could see the remnants of an old stone wall that once bordered the town. He wondered if it was for defence or just to find a use for the stones farmers pulled from their fields. The road to the estate was long and winding with large conifers whose branches reached over the ditch, threatening to graze any vehicle that wandered too close. After some time, the car came to a halt before a stone and iron fence, and in its centre, a large iron gate was propped open. A heavy chain lay hanging from one of the cross members, and on the other gate was a larger padlock.

Will felt it safe to assume there was little to no electronic security on the premises, which, to him, was a mixed blessing. On the one hand, he lacked the benefit of built-in cameras to watch the place for any unusual happening. But, on the other hand, he would be able to work without being watched himself. Either way, it was of little concern for him as Richard would be coming the next day with his equipment, which was far superior and sensitive to any security camera.

The giant mansion was already in view, looming in the background like some foreboding thing that glared at him from its many eye-socket windows.

What a grand palace, he thought to himself as he took in the eerie majesty of the structure. The house looked as though it was constructed of red brick and grey stone, with lichens and moulds growing and the course texture of the variety of gargoyles that jutted from the roof and walls, displaying their weathered colours from years of traversing water from the mansion.

A variation of small turrets extended from the walls and corners of the building to house stairwells and rooms with sliding bay doors that opened onto small balconies. Big bay windows looked out onto the orchard, vineyard, and gorgeous gardens like giant glass eyes with heavy curtains drawn to the sides. They let in just enough light to allow one to see in. On one side of the mansion, above the window, the walls were blackened by what looked like mould or soot from a fire, whose heat and flames had scorched it. The other side of the house was obscured by vines and ivy that crawled up the walls and jutting stones to hang over the windows like tattered curtains. Luscious gardens were well maintained all about the structure, and as Will gazed in wonderment, he noticed the statue of an angel bordering the forest. It, too, was mainly concealed in ivy but could very well be one of many headstones in a family cemetery.

Will approached the giant wooden doors to meet a lady standing in wait dressed in what could have been a server's uniform. She had a bland expression on her face that slightly returned the smile as he introduced himself.

"Yes, we have been in expectation of your arrival, Mr. Stilton. My name is Lucy Bristol, but everyone calls me Broom as I assist and overlook the upkeep of the Law estate."

Will's expression became serious as he nodded in acknowledgement, mostly because he felt he should.

"If you will gather your effects, Mr. Stilton, I shall show you to your room." Without a word, Will collected his luggage and carryall and followed Lucy through the heavy doors.

The house was elegantly decorated; the decorum was reflective of the era the mansion's exterior personified. The building opened into a large foyer with robust, dark wood banisters that crept up the walls to meet at a large landing overlooking everything. The ceiling was high, and a stained glass portrait window peered down, casting its rainbow light onto the floor with the reflections from the grand chandelier.

Will's jaw dropped slightly as he took in the décor. He was in for a treat if this is what the entrance boasted, and he could hardly wait to see his room.

"Where may I find Mrs. Law?" he queried.

"You don't, Mr. Stilton. She will find you when it is fitting for her to do so."

He nodded in acknowledgement. He was slightly annoyed at her response. He wasn't one to be kept waiting and found himself entertaining the idea that this was a display of power, though he didn't really understand why. He followed Lucy down the corridor until they came upon his room.

"Here is where you will be for the duration of your stay, Mr. Stilton," she said, stepping to one side and allowing him in the room, keeping herself on the other side of the threshold. "I would give you a key for your door, but they had a habit of locking themselves, and so Mrs. Law had all the interior locks removed, with some exceptions of other rooms, of course."

Will turned to meet her gaze. It was quite stern and demanding of his obedience.

"If it has a lock, Mr. Stilton, it is not meant to be opened." And with that, she turned and left with a reminder that dinner would be served at seven o clock sharp, and he was expected to wear something befitting such an occasion.

"Oh, and one other thing."

Will turned suddenly to find her back at the doorway.

"I don't believe in ghosts, Mr. Stilton, but something peculiar has befallen this place, and I have been here a long time." And she was off once again.

Will's room reflected the foyer with all the delicacies of the Victorian era. His bed was large and had decorated mahogany posts on each corner, accenting the stone fireplace with mahogany inlay. Soot and ash spilled from its gaping maw, and chunks of mostly incinerated wood lay strewn inside, but there was no dried wood stacked in the old firewood caddy. A variety of small tables, vases, and trinkets decorated the room. Some modern touches stood out: a gliding rocking chair rested in one corner near the new windows that overlooked the vineyard and garden. He hung his shirts and pants in the closet, then took stock of his handbag once more as he did before he departed: an EMF meter, two recorders for EVPs, his trusty compass, a digital camera, as well as a regular 8mm SLR film camera, an infrared thermometer, his torch, and a pad and pens. When Will had finished unpacking, he took it upon himself to tour the grounds, starting with the garden that demonstrated such elegance and beauty it seemed almost surreal to walk through.

Fountains and small stream-fed ponds abounded with luscious flora and stone walkways with trimmed hedges and solitary sitting areas with trellises.

"Hello!" came a voice.

Will turned to meet a young woman. She was wearing a sleeved shirt and overalls adorned with smudges of dirt.

"You're the paranormal investigator everyone has heard about?"

He nodded, smiling. "That I am." He extended his hand. "Will Stilton of the Stilton Paranormal Research Institute."

She returned the smile and graciously accepted the gesture. "Saraphima."

Her hand was soft for a gardener's and cool to the touch, but her grip was remarkably strong. Saraphima stepped back, studying Will as though he had piqued her interest on some level. There was a haunting familiarity about her, and he knew what it was.

She had shoulder-length brown hair that ended in wavy curls, brown eyes, and a cute button nose. Will estimated her to be five feet in height, and if he had to guess, he'd say she was between her late twenties and early thirties.

"I suppose you're wondering if there is anything that happens in the garden?"

Will was amused. "I will be. I was more or less taking in the sights." He gestured all around him in the garden.

"Why, thank you, Mr. Stilton. These gardens are my home and what you see are the fruits of my labour," she said with pride. The garden was indeed vast and wonderful to the point of enchantment. It extended from the drive across the front of the mansion, disappearing around the building and bordering a gnarly orchard far in the distance. From the front of the mansion, it reached beyond the length of the drive to a forest of tall deciduous trees. Will was no forester, but from where he stood, he could make out beeches, maples, oaks, and hickories. It was getting close to fall, and the oaks were turning their vibrant shade of red, mixing with the yellow hues and the lighter shades of red from the maples and hickories. Many birds lingered in their large branches and danced about the garden before making their migration. Dragonflies buzzed about, competing with swallows for what insects remained. There was a focal point, a tall three-tier fountain that babbled and splashed as the water spouted from the top and tumbled to the pool below. Its character was weathered and dreary in contrast to the vibrancy of the flowers, with all their colourful hues scattered throughout the garden in ornate planters.

Will breathed deeply of the fresh air, then turned his attention back to Saraphima. "I have been informed that Mrs. Law will be seeing me at her leisure, so since you bring it up, have you seen anything? In the garden?"

Saraphima smiled as though she were purposefully being coy and pondered for a moment as if she had something to divulge but was weighing if she should. Then her expression changed. She looked at him, and Will imagined she was harbouring some sinful secret and relishing the moment.

"They say there is a woman that wanders these gardens." Her eyes locked on to his. "I hear she roams about freely. Night or day, it doesn't matter. I hear she's an enchantress, looking for the love she never had."

Will's eyebrows raised. This sounded more like an urban legend than a ghost story.

"I also hear that she used to work at this very estate."

Will was amused and was more than willing to entertain her story. "And have you seen this spectre you speak of?"

She waved her hand in the air as if dismissing the query. "Nah, I haven't seen anything, and I'm usually too busy to notice everything. I've been here for what feels like a lifetime!" She let out a sigh and paused.

"Well, it was a pleasure to meet you, Mr. Stilton. I hope to see you again."

His smile hadn't wavered. "I am pretty sure you will."

She returned the smile and turned, disappearing behind the cedar hedge. Will felt his heart flutter then sink into his chest, pulling on his throat to the point of constriction, but he managed to maintain his composure. Saraphima looked so much like Brynn, his fiance once upon a time. That had ended in tragedy. The resemblance was uncanny: her brown shoulder-length hair that ended in wavy curls, her dark eyes, her button nose, hell, even her bloody five-foot stature.

Memories chased each other through his mind. He recalled their happiness, Brynn's smile that so resembled this gardener's and the way she looked at him. Memories he had so well suppressed had come flooding back. Will recalled her face that fateful morning, how he'd kissed her cheek, her lips, savouring the precious moment before going to work. He remembered her eyes, saturated with tears, when he came home. The plethora of smells that had lingered in the hospital as doctors ran a myriad of tests. Will recalled telling her how beautiful she was when her hair had fallen out. He could still feel the texture of her skin as she withered away, cradling her frail, gaunt frame, kissing her temple all the while. He had so regretted not marrying her on her deathbed so she could at least go as his wife and he, her husband. He didn't care how morbid that might have been. He recalled his final farewell as she drew her last breath, taken by the cancer. In this moment, everything he'd fallen in love with was mirrored by this young woman.

Later that evening, Will accompanied Mrs. Law in the dining room. It was just as elegant and ornate as the rest of the house, with a grand, dark walnut table that spanned most of the room's length. Tall windows to his left looked out into the front of the mansion, and to his right, finely painted tapestries adorned the wall. At the far end of the room was a large stone fireplace accented by a sizable wooden mantle. He wore his casual, brown corduroy single-breasted blazer that he always wore to new hauntings or meetings with clients. Often he'd heard the comments that he resembled some university professor, which was confirmation enough that he looked the part of a professional presenter.

"Good evening, Mr. Stilton," started Mrs. Law as she entered the room with Lucy in tow. She wore an elegant cream blouse with buttons done snug to her neck and pinned with a brooch. The blouse's tight fit followed the curvature of her slim body, billowing at the wrists. Her black skirt was almost as form revealing, tightly bound at her waist with a clasp and gradually flaring out at her ankles. Its pleats made it wide enough that she could take full strides without restriction. Her hair was tied tightly in a bun at the back of her head, and her tone was hard and very direct. Her demeanour befitted someone who would command an empire, and she demanded authority.

"Good evening," he said in reply as he straightened in his chair.

She dispensed with the pleasantries and got right to her point. "Let me be frank, Mr. Stilton. I do not believe in ghosts, spirits, or things that go bump in the night."

She paused for a second, but Will had been down this controversial road many times and did not give her the satisfaction of any reaction.

"I find the idea of the wandering souls utterly incongruous. When we die, we are dead. End of story. It is not factual for one to come back from the earth."

Too often, Will had dealt with people who didn't believe in the paranormal or supernatural and yet hired his and his brother's services, typically as a last resort. Unfortunately, these were also the kind of people who were most adamant about telling them how to do their jobs. He suddenly wished Richard were here with him. He had a much higher tolerance for clients of this mindset, and he usually helped him keep his cool.

"Then my presence here is of the utmost hypocrisy," he rebutted with a low hard tone. This was not the meeting he was looking forward to. "If you are so adamant in this view, why hire my services?"

She leaned forward as if she were enjoying this, as if it were a game of wits. "Because, Mr. Stilton, you have published literature in the field. You debunk poltergeist phenomena as a disingenuous haunt. According to you, it is the environment manipulated by children who have entered the pubescent phase of their lives. They are a product of telekinesis. You also suggest that it's a cause of an environment being manipulated by a strong electromagnetic field. For example, an aquifer running under a house or ley lines. Even geological activity can cause such occurrences, manifestations easily presumed to be a poltergeist infestation. You discuss an 'intelligent haunt' versus an 'electromagnet imprint left in an environment,' and you discuss how the spectre can actually interact with the people and environment around it whilst the latter is merely a repetition, residual energy carrying out the same task over and over."

Will smiled and the thought of her reading his work. "A phantom," he uttered.

Mrs. Law leaned forward with her hands clasped together on the table. "You argue the authenticity of still-frame film photographs versus digital, as they are not so easily manipulated, so the film photo is indeed more genuine. Case in point, the Newby Church spectre, the Brown Lady of Raynham Hall. Need I go on, Mr. Stilton?"

Will shook his head.

"I have also procured a great many other well-published documented cases crediting yourself, your brother, and the institute." She placed her hand on a stack of folders with photocopied pages neatly spilling out of them, colourful finger tabs separating each case as if ready to be plucked one by one if need be. "The scientific community respects your opinions, and it seems that ghost enthusiasts look up to you, even though you represent the human embodiment of an oxymoron; you're both a believer and a sceptic. Oh, the trials you must face sometimes."

Will smiled a small, almost cocky grin. He didn't know if she intended to be insulting or sympathetic.

"You have also been quoted as stating, 'demons are ambiguous…'"

Another smile from Will. "I have yet to meet one," he replied.

Mrs. Law retorted with a satisfactory head nod. "You will find that I am quite familiar with you and your work. You and your brother own your own firm specializing in the paranormal. You have spent your life trying to prove their existence. In short, Mr. Stilton, you're the best at proving their nonexistence."

She nodded to Lucy, who made her way to Will and placed a bulging envelope on the table before him, then returned to her station to the left of Mrs. Law and just behind her.

"This is half of what I am willing to pay for your services. Should you be successful in this venture, the second will be most substantial."

Will eyed the envelope for a moment then accepted it, taking note of his new client's satisfactory expression.

Will took a mental note of the weight of the envelope as he slipped it into the inside pocket of his blazer. "I cannot rid a house of ghosts. I help authenticate the existence of paranormal phenomena with what evidence I can produce or lack thereof. I'm in the business of believing in it, Mrs. Law."

"And do you believe in it, Mr. Stilton?" She was studying him carefully.

"I have my reservations," he replied. Will then looked at Lucy, who was trying to read him as much as Mrs. Law was. He did believe in the paranormal and the unexplained. He'd seen more than his fair share of phenomena that would turn any sceptic into a believer, but a vast number of paranormal occurrences could be explained away with an environmental influence, or any other influence, that may affect the environment around the investigators. Science is in the business of facts and certainties, and this is why the "science" of the paranormal and modern science will always clash.

"I believe there is the possibility of an underground water source like a fast-moving aquifer that would amplify the kinetic and thermal energy, therefore, increasing the potential paranormal activity in the area. A hydrogeologist would have been brought in if that were the case, as there would be a tremendous amount of water flowing." Will took another sip of wine.

"I believe we're close to the Tees-Exe line, geologically; it divides the highland and the lowland regions, marking the soft low-lying topography in the South East and the hard more mountainous region in the North West. I know it's not a fault line, but there is the potential for a hotbed of geological activity that could cause high amounts of kinetic energy. This, too, could heighten all phenomena that could be written off as paranormal or supernatural, to start."

She regarded him for a moment. "I am well aware of my location, Mr. Stilton."

Will continued, "If you so fervently believe you don't have a paranormal infestation, then what do you have, Mrs. Law? A geological conundrum?" Will asked plainly as he sipped his wine, then looked at the glass as if studying the liquor. What an interesting taste for a red wine.

Mrs. Law took a bite of her dinner then placed her silverware gently on her plate. "Skeletons, perhaps Mr. Stilton. This place has become foreboding and forlorn with the superstitions of weak-minded people. I, however, am much harder to convince. I don't believe in ghosts, but unfortunately, those in my employ do, the whole bloody town, for that matter.

The workers here talk, Mr. Stilton, and right now, there are rumours of ghosts haunting the grounds. Many of my hands have left for employment elsewhere, while some have fled in fear, ranting and raving about what you call the paranormal."

Will could not contain the smirk forming.

"Which brings you to me." Mrs. Law nodded. "I want this put to an end. I cannot afford to run a business if my employees keep decamping. What I'm willing to pay you is minor compared to what I stand to lose. So do what you do best. Look for ghosts, prove me wrong, and in doing so, prove that the superstitions of those in my employ are ill-founded. One other thing, Lucy told you about the locked doors?"

He nodded.

"I trust your curiosity will not get the better of you. Secondly, you will report to Lucy or me each evening or upon request. And, Mr. Stilton, I will undoubtedly be the most sceptical individual you have ever met, is that clear?"

Will nodded, confirming he understood her instruction.

"Very good. I look forward to our meetings in the coming days ahead. She dabbed the corners of her mouth with her serviette, then rose from the table, Will following suit. Mrs. Law paused as she walked past Will and glanced at the half-drunk glass of wine.

"Enjoy the wine, Mr. Stilton. It's from my private reserve of a particular fermentation. You will find it is quite interesting on the pallet." With that, she exited the room with Lucy in tow.

Will sat back down. Grasping the wine glass, he sniffed at it again and took another sip. Definitely interesting. He then turned his attention to the dinner he hadn't touched yet and guessed it to be grouse. Suddenly he felt hungry. As he ate, he pondered his experience with the Law estate so far and the character of his new employer. A sense of uneasiness came over him. This was going to be a trying and potentially taxing venture.

CHAPTER THREE

FIRST NIGHT

Will welcomed the smooth taste of scotch as he sat in a lounge chair, looking out the window over the gardens and into the vineyard. It was getting dark, and the sky was a tapestry of reds and crimson hues. Shadows stretched across the ground as if ready to embrace the dark. He counted the money that Mrs. Law had given him and returned it to the envelope. It was double what he normally charged. She was making this venture lucrative for him, which brought its own suspicions, but he quickly dismissed them. He turned his attention to the garden, hoping to catch the image of Saraphima again in the fading light. A smile crossed his lips as he took another sip, savouring the smooth burning sensation. She was so much like Brynn, whom he missed dearly, but she was gone, and he'd come to terms with that so many years ago. There was such a familiarity that he felt comfortable around her. Will took another sip that emptied the glass.

He'd better get a move on if he wanted to get some pictures and touring done tonight before it grew too late. He had set himself a curfew so that he would be better rested for the following night when Richard came. How he was looking forward to seeing Rich again. As he set down his glass and rose from the desk, glancing out the window, he noticed Saraphima entering the courtyard of the garden. She was still wearing her coveralls with her plaid shirt, but he was unable to make out any dirt stains given the light. His heart involuntarily fluttered as he watched her walk to the fountain and tend to the lilies. The garden of lilies with their hues of red, white, and yellow enveloped the fountain's base. The babbling water seemed alive. It was an enchanting array of colour and movement. He almost cringed when she glanced up, taking notice of him. A smile crossed her lips, and she waved.

Will returned the gesture then stepped back from the window. "If there was but one saving grace for this place...," he mumbled to himself as he gathered his things: camera, infrared thermometer, electromagnetic field meter, and of course, his trusty compass. Slipping on a light coat, he filled its pockets with the effects as he made for the door.

Meandering through the courtyard, he strolled along manicured walking paths of fine crushed stone that opened up into a wide area of mossy flagstone, bearing features such as massive stone planters. An array of flowers and shrubbery sprouted from urn-shaped vessels, displaying their colours like massive potted peacocks. The furled edges of the pots were concealed by the branches of the shrubbery, dangling like wooden fingers adorned with greenery as if trying to conceal the many weathered cracks in the vessels.

Will made his way to the gardener, plucking at the lilies in the water at the base of the fountain.

"Hello, Mr. William," she said avidly as he approached.

He returned her smile. "Will will do. And good evening to you, Miss Saraphima."

"Are you on the infamous hunt?" she queried, looking at the array of gadgets poking out from his jacket pockets.

Will looked up at the sun-setting sky, then back to her. "I am." He took a seat on the fountain's edge. "But I am also curious. Do you always work so late?"

Saraphima finished placing the lilies in her basket and, cradling it in both hands, straightened up. "I don't. I finished work a while ago. But I propagated these lilies, and now I'm taking some for my place."

Will just sat there looking at her with the same adoring eyes he used to look at Brynn with, then he glanced to the ground and back at her. "Do all employees live on the estate?"

She smiled. "Some have families in town and commute each day."

He nodded. "So, where, to your knowledge, is most of the 'activity' located?"

She laughed. "I was waiting for you to just come out and ask." She paused to compose herself. "It happens everywhere, from what I hear."

His expression turned to one of curiosity. Will straightened and turned so now his whole upper torso was facing her. "So, you hear?"

She looked at him inquisitively. "Yes, I have not seen anything, Mr. Will. I only hear stories." With that, she turned. "Have a good night, Mr. Will," she said as she disappeared behind some large yew trees.

Will sat at the fountain's edge for a moment listening to the soothing chant of the water trickling and falling into the pool. His thoughts quickly turned to his unfinished glass of scotch in his room. "The sooner I finish this walk about the grounds, the sooner I get to finish my drink." He chuckled to himself. The bottle was not what he came here to find but the very thing he should avoid. With that, he started through the garden, snapping pictures with both his infrared and regular film cameras. As Will meandered about, he could not help but feel a heaviness in the air. Not only did the estate look old, but it felt old also. Soon the moon was floating in the sky, casting its luminescence like a ghostly ship haunting the sea. Will started making his way back to the mansion. The lights from its many sconces spilling from the windows with an almost sinister glow gave it an otherworldly atmosphere. He pushed open the large wooden doors. The wrought iron hinges creaked and cried under the door's weight, reverberating through the massive foyer.

Will took it upon himself to tour the mansion's corridors. They were winsome with a Gothic Victorian air. Large paintings of family lost, relatives and friends, or at least what he presumed to be so. Every hallway felt very long and neverending as he continued to test what doors he could open and what he couldn't. Most of the doors opened, revealing to him their secrets of hidden bedrooms, playrooms, living rooms, and what seemed to be a nursery. It was all enchanting. Never before had he been in such a setting.

He found his way to the scullery and then the kitchen. What was once intricately decorated in its Gothic Victorian charm had been vastly updated and was now cold and hard as stainless steel replaced the old wooden countertops and dated appliances. The cupboard doors were still thick dark wood carved with their intricacies. Pots and pans hung above the island, their distorted silhouettes reflecting in the shiny surface. On the wall was a magnet bearing the polished blades of knives and cleavers. He snapped a few infrared pictures as he manoeuvred from one side of the kitchen to the other. Then turning for the door, there came the clatter of metal on metal, ringing behind him. Will spun about, his eyes wide with anticipation as he examined the kitchen that was now silent. He glared hard at the suspended pots and pans in expectancy, but they remained silent and unmoving. He knew what he had heard, and there was a potential environmental explanation, such as it was cold enough for the metal to contract, causing the cookware to shift. Or he unwittingly brushed against one of the suspended cookware pieces as he walked by. But surely what he touched would be swaying, but the room remained still. A touch of disappointment passed through him as he turned to make his way from the kitchen when he felt a sudden wisp of chill brush the back of his neck. Will spun about, training his eyes around the room, intently examining the darkest shadows, watching them in their deceiving forms. His eyes darted from the shadows to the hanging cookware and back to the shadows again.

He pulled an infrared thermometer from the satchel he carried on his side and directed it around the room. A red laser sight pulsed into the darkest pitch with no illumination as though the darkness was consuming it. The temperature remained a constant twenty-one degrees Celsius. He was satisfied enough and tired from the flight in. All he wanted to do was sit and relax for a moment with his glass of scotch. Today was a satisfactory start. He got to meet Mrs. Law, and now he and his brother had been charged with the task of proving her wrong. Nope, today went as good as expected, but the real investigation would commence once Richard arrived.

Will made his way into his room, where he removed his flat hat, emptied his coat pockets, and placed the contents on the bed in a nice fashion. Then he removed from his carryall a blank book and a nice writing pen and sat at the writing desk by the window where the bottle of peaty nectar resided for now. There was a hollow *thupe* as he uncorked the scotch, poured a small nip, and began the arduous task of recording his findings for the day. The more he recalled his meeting with Mrs. Law, the more he pondered the case he was now tasked with.

"'I don't believe in ghosts. When we die, we die, that's it."

He took a sip. He'd heard that before. It was what followed.

"Prove me wrong, Mr. Stilton."

That was unique, as no one had ever charged him with that before.

Downing the remainder of his scotch, his face tightened and winced as the smooth burning sensation felt satisfying as it went down. He was tired. His eyes were heavy, and his head was starting to slump.

Will managed to pull himself into bed to succumb to the weight of the heavy sheets, his eyes barely held open. He fell asleep to the soothing rhythmic sound of the rocking chair as it started to sway back and forth.

CHAPTER FOUR

RICHARD

Will awoke to the rumbling and crunching of tires on gravel. With eyes still shut, he reached for his watch, only to grasp the cold hard arm of the glider rocker beside his bed. It was freezing cold as if he had grasped a block of ice. Will retracted his hand from the cold that shocked him into alertness and sent chills coursing through his body. Sitting up abruptly, he glared at the chair for a moment. Rays of light from the morning sun beamed through the window and came to rest on the glider rocker. It appeared to be warm and inviting had it not mysteriously been pressed against the bed.

B Will hesitated, then placed his hand on it once again. The chair was not as cold on the second touch and was quite firmly pressed against the bed. Pulling himself from the sanctity of his sheets, Will noticed the track marks on the floor from where it originally rested in the corner of the room. They were quite deep as if from years of wear. How hadn't he noticed this before?

Will made his way to the window over the desk, his eyes not deviating from the glider rocker as if he were expecting it to abruptly slide back into place. Will turned to look out the window to see Richard with the company van come to a halt in the drive. He turned his attention back to the chair. Annoyance quickly welled up within him, not so much that his chair was somehow dragged across the floor but at the idea that someone may have thought it funny to play a trick and was stealthy enough not to wake him up.

And on more than one occasion, he thought to himself, studying the depth of the grooves in the floor as he grabbed the chair and dragged it back to its resting spot in the corner of the room.

Will quickly got himself dressed, disregarding his shaggy morning beard. He turned before leaving the room and looked around at its entirety for a moment. "Leave my shit alone," he said to the air before closing the door behind him.

"Don't rule out all possibilities," he said to himself as he made his way down the hall.

The more you cannot disprove something, the more you are actually proving it, was something Richard always told him. *You have to be accepting and open-minded with all possibilities when you're in a haunted situation, Will. Otherwise, every little sound or shape-shifting shadow will be a ghost in your mind, and you won't be able to differentiate fiction from signs and symptoms of a true haunting.*

Will smiled, remembering his brother's lecture years back when they first started their venture together. Will was already very much aware of this, but Richard always felt that he had to remind him. Will knew all too well he'd chase his own shadow, thinking it was a ghost back then, but years of debunking cases had definitely hardened him. As much as Will was still a believer, he was now equally a sceptic, and what was once advice had become an unwritten rule.

He very much enjoyed his investigations with his brother. Over the years, he or Richard had started leading small teams of researchers individually, taking on separate cases. So when opportunities arose for the duo to work together, they both enjoyed it immensely.

Richard leaned over the dash, glaring out the window at the massive mansion with its eerie presence. It felt as though it were looming over him with foreboding intent, trying to instil fear in him to scare the investigator away before he could dissect its nighttime phenomena.

"Bloody hell!" he uttered as he sat back then made his way out of the vehicle, standing with his hands on his hips staring back at the imposing, chilling, austere estate. "I've seen worse!" he said aloud, in part because he actually hadn't and partly because it did make him feel better.

Making his way up to the concrete steps, Richard couldn't help but feel like he was walking into the belly of the beast. Before the large wooden door, he noticed an older lady standing on the top step as if in expectancy with an expression of annoyance. It was as though he should have arrived hours ago. Richard was taken off guard. He'd not seen her exit the building nor come up the steps. Had she been there the whole time?

Despite her gloomy appearance, his happy eyes glittered. He'd always been good at diffusing potentially awkward situations with his charm and wit before they had a chance to transpire, and he felt this particular moment heeded all he could currently muster. He tried to put out some charm in greeting the stern-looking woman, but her expression failed to alter. Her demeanour did not change, and her eyes remained cold, fixed on him. He suddenly felt uncomfortable standing a few steps below her.

"I am sorry," he said as he removed his sunglasses. "Was I expected at an earlier time?" He looked at his watch. "It's half past one now. I left the office around nine and stopped for a bite."

Her eyes met his. "Your time of arrival was not specified."

He smiled. "Good!" he said cheerfully. Richard was not about to put up with arrogant games. He had dealt with people like this in the past, and it had proven to be a nuisance. They were closed-minded and unaccepting.

"I can assume you are Mr. Stilton's brother." It was more of a statement than a query.

"I am," he said pleasantly, making his way to where she stood to tower over her.

Richard leaned slightly over to look her directly in her unwavering icy eyes. "You may take me to see Mr. William or Mrs. Law at this juncture."

It must have been somewhat intimidating for her as she stammered back on her heels, trying to maintain eye contact and realizing just how tall he really was.

Richard took a modicum of delight and was about to ask if she were alright when Will exited the large doors.

"Mr. Stilton!" said Richard, returning to his pleasant tone as he reached out.

"Cut it out, Richard," replied Will, shaking his brother's hand. He was well aware of Richard's antics. A somewhat relieved smile crossed his cheeks as they shook. He already sensed this was not going to be an easy case, and having his brother with him was comforting.

"I can show Richard where he will be sleeping tonight, Lucy, if that is fine with you. We can better prepare if we start now."

She passed them, making her way through the door, refusing to acknowledge the tall black man beside her. His happy eyes did not leave her.

"Very well," she said as she closed the door that shut with a loud *clunk*.

"What a bitch," Richard announced and turned, half-hoping she could hear it.

Will simply smiled, then headed to the van, and Richard followed. As he walked, Will began to describe his meeting with Mrs. Law and expressed his desire to get this case over with so he could take a vacation.

Richard laughed at Will's disheartening over the case. Even though he was rough about its proposal, he had seen that his brother had wanted to go, but not at the drop of a letter.

That night, Richard, with Will's help, set up his equipment in all the rooms Will had shown him. Their base of operations was in Will's room, as it was far larger and had a desk by the window. It was more accommodating overall, as though his room had served an alternate purpose, but he could only speculate as to what, if that were indeed the case. His guess would have been an office or a meeting room, given its proximity through the window. One could watch all who entered and exited the estate.

Richard was far superior with his tech than Will. He stayed behind to monitor two computer screens that gave him video feed from various cameras, including one he taped into Will's flat hat. Richard had wired his brother into instruments that would detect rapid changes in the environment, such as quick shifts of hot to cold and variations in electromagnetic convulsions, should they manoeuvre through the corridors and rooms of the seemingly musty mansion.

It was getting dark and a little chilly outside and a three-quarter moon soon illuminated the rooms and hallways of the estate. Large trees and statues cast deformed shadows across the garden and against the house, some creeping in through the old windows whose panes were distorted and warped from the years of elements. Amidst the garden, little cameras could be seen motionless, and at times, panning back and forth to capture what intruded their line of sight. The tiny cameras swept the rooms, corridors, and garden, flickering ever so slightly as he changed their view from infrared and back to a normal colour frame. Richard was everywhere he wanted to be at once as long as he stayed still. He was camped out in luxury and very much liked staying put while Will did most of the footwork.

Will silently stalked through the house, his camera at the ready. Before him, he held an EMF, taking readings of the environment around him, checking to see if there was a spike in the meter. A compass around his neck gently swayed against his chest, always drawn to the magnetic north unless otherwise disturbed by unseen forces such as EMFs, causing it to spin sporadically. An infrared thermometer hung at his belt with a small digital camera, and strapped over his shoulder was an infrared camera. Nothing out of the ordinary, just a creepy mansion with its ornate sconces jutting from the walls. With their stagnant illumination, there was no vibrancy or warmth to their light as they illuminated the worn wainscotting in the corridors. Bits of wallpaper peeled away from the top of the wainscotting, frail and fragile, but it still held firm up to the ceiling. Parts of the carpet appeared almost threadbare, and that was where the floorboards beneath creaked the most.

An earpiece kept him in constant communication with Richard, who was perched in Will's bedroom, keeping avid eyes on the monitors. The sound of Will's shoes on the old hardwood floor was the only noise in the quiet hallways. Will pressed forward cautiously as a predator stalks its prey, though he was growing more sceptical of the lore of the prey that stalked this estate. They had managed to speak with one of the lead orchardists earlier that day, and he obliged Will and Richard with some descriptive details of the stories that circulated through the workers. His adopted brother, in his professional manner, was becoming more excited for the hunt, taking in what the hands had to say. But as Will took notes, he was more amused by their naive disillusions than anything else.

He expected to find nothing in this investigation, but like every other investigation, he did harbour hope. He'd seen enough to warrant that. This also made the exposure of true paranormal influence that much more exciting. This mindset he'd adopted over the years helped keep him from "chasing shadows." He would always be a believer, even if he was in the "business of believing," and even if he was entering every case as a sceptic. If he wasn't sceptical, then every breeze that blew, every chill in the air, every dust or moisture on a camera lens, anything that had an air of abnormality, would be written off as paranormal when, in fact, it had a logical explanation. Shit! Richard could fart, and he could write it off as a fucking demon!

Ornate Victorian brass wall sconces, a product of their era, illuminated small pockets of light like old street lamps lining a deserted road. Will walked, slipping between light and darkness as he slowly meandered onward. At times his thoughts and concentration were interrupted with the crackle of static in his earpiece and Richard's voice making small talk or directing the camera on his hat. Sometimes, Richard instructed Will to turn in directions where he could see and identify what possible entities he may or may not have briefly captured on his infrared scope.

In their communications, Will spoke slowly and clearly, allowing Richard to record any of their findings or near misses in his log of their minutes, writing down anything he felt suspicious or needed extra attention. It saved them hours of watching the videos over and over. They watched them anyway, as certain frames would have to be dissected or called for further attention.

Kshhk

"This place really maintains the century in which it was built!" announced Richard through the earpiece. "Looks as though it would have been built mid-to-late eighteen hundreds."

Kshhk

Will ignored his brother for the time being. He was transfixed on the fluttering light that seemed to suddenly affect a number of the wall sconces leading down the hallway. His breathing became heavier, but he wasn't afraid. He could feel the moistness on his skin appear. His heart rate became elevated, and his hair stood up, all signs and symptoms of anxiety and the possible introduction of some real paranormal contact, or perhaps it was merely the mental stigma of being in a creepy old mansion at night.

If Richard were talking, he could no longer hear him. His eyes were set ahead around a bend in the hallway where the light was faltering, and the darkness was consuming. Slowly and steadily, he moved forward, pausing to check his EMF meter for any fluctuations in the atmosphere around him. It was normal. The electromagnetic field from the sconces had elevated the meter, and taking that into account, he was not concerned about any.

He then lifted the compass that hung around his neck and was taken aback. The needle was spinning sporadically right to left. He wanted to be excited about the situation, but he wrote it off as nervousness for what the darkness held around the bend. He regained his composure, stood straight, and took in a deep breath. He had seen this on many occasions where faulty, poor, or old wiring caused electrical malfunctions throughout an entire house. The only difference here was the situation, which was much eerier than most modern houses he typically inspected.

Richard set down his Thermos cap of coffee as he watched the computer monitors flicker from their picture to static. At times, the screens were distorted, the images on the monitor twisting and contorting. Once, the camera on Will's hat appeared to be level with his feet, and everything was wound like a saturated wash cloth.

Setting functions on the keyboards had no effect; all the connections were in their proper places and secure. He had been reduced to tapping the monitors, which evolved to holding one side firm and slapping the other in a futile attempt to regain his pictures. He knew his equipment inside and out, and never before had he seen anything like this happen. He suddenly paused. The vapour of his own breath crept up his cheeks, kissing his skin with its moist warmth and evaporating about him.

His skin began to tingle, and the room felt dreary. His breathing became heavy as he slowly scanned the shadows that crept from the darkest corners to reach for the light from his computers. He grabbed his coffee, which, surprisingly, was still warm and took a large sip, feeling the rush of liquid upon his lips and down his esophagus—a rush of warmth upon his tongue that was growing stiff from the abruptly cool air.

Just then, there was a creak at the door, a whimper within the wood, distant pleas of mercy and a cry of sorrow, and then silence befell everywhere. So deathly silent that the air became still about Richard, and he actually felt afraid, as if deep inside he was reduced to a fearing child. The door moaned again, only louder as if its very wooden fibres were protesting.

Richard stood, still holding his coffee. He slowly started to make his way toward the door when the creaking of unsettled wood vibrated through the floor. He turned to where he could hear the mechanics of a glider rocker swaying to and fro, slightly thumping on the wall behind it, its rhythm steady. Richard made his way to the corner of the room; placing his hand on the back of the chair, he drew it back in shock, shuddering.

The rocking came to a halt, and the chair was icy cold to the touch, an unnatural cold that seemed to bite the skin and seep deep into his hand. It settled in his body as if to pierce his very being. He'd felt cold such as this before in transparent spots in other hauntings, but this was particularly intense.

The door moaned again, a hollow ache and pain that resounded through the room like a dull echo. Richard turned from the chair and made his way to the door, slowly drawing closer to the disembodied cry that resounded through the dense wood.

He crept past his computers, their dull light casting small shards of shadow on the floor and wall, until the door was before him. It moaned again, dull and low. Slowly, he reached out and placed his hand on the old wood. It was wet and surprisingly warm, thick and viscous to the touch. The cries and moaning ceased as his hand came to rest on the wet wood. Richard pulled his hand from the door and reached for the light switch. The lights came to life, and his computers flickered and returned to their camera views of the estate. He looked down at his hand, his eyes went wide, and he stumbled backward in shock, then his eyes darted to the door. Blood trickled down his wrist and dripped onto the floor. It poured from the door's woodgrain, saturating it, dripping, running down and pooling on the floor before him.

Richard fell to the floor, grasping for his microphone, but Will was already there. Richard looked up at his brother standing in the doorway, and the heavy door swung open, smearing the blood on the floor. Will turned white as he glanced at the pooled liquid and then at his brother's hand.

"What happened, Richard? Holy shit! Are you okay?" There was excitement in his voice muddled with concern.

"I'm fine." He was shaking from the experience.

"I tried to contact you on the headset, but you failed to respond. I can see why. The lights were flickering in the hallways, and my EMF was pulsing slightly rather than spiking with the electrical surges, so I passed them off as just that, electrical surges, and decided to come back. Glad I did too!"

"Do you have any idea what I just experienced, Will?! What this is?" Richard glared at him, his sweat dripping off his brow and neck, saturating the collar and chest of his shirt. "Come in and close the door."

He was practically yelling. He hoped that they had not awoken any of the permanent residents of this estate. The walls appeared thin, showing their age, weary of the load they had to bear for so long, the kind of walls that secrets and rumours would slip past or through to filter through the weary abode.

Will closed the door gently. As he did so, he stared at the bloody figure oozing from the woodgrain. His eyes widened, and his jaw went slack as he glared at the very human figure. He gasped as he ran his fingertips down the grain, the warm viscous plasma pooling around his fingers. "It's a form of ectoplasm," he said, his voice shaking.

"It is a residual byproduct of a paranormal entity." Richard smiled as he stated this, as though quoting from text.

Will stumbled backwards, careful not to step in the puddle on the floor and started taking infrared photographs of the phenomena in his very bedroom.

"The computers started to malfunction. They were distorted and static. I lost all video and communication before this happened." Richard paused for a moment, then raised a finger toward the glider rocker in the corner of the room. "That chair started to move of its own accord. It was rocking back and forth, thumping on the wall, and when I placed my hand on it to stop, the motion, it was icy cold!"

He watched Will navigate to the chair. He placed his hand on the back of it.

"Hmm. Yes, this chair... Mrs. Law is such a sceptic; I don't know how I will explain any of this to her." He paused for a moment, with Richard watching attentively. "Or perhaps I won't, not just yet."

Will turned to his brother. "Mrs. Law, for starters, is a grumpy old hag who looks and acts like she just drank of glass of her own piss."

Richard laughed as he turned his attention back to his computers. Then he turned to face Will again. "Why don't you get the film developed first, then you can present everything at once," he said. "We had an occurrence tonight, nothing more. Inconclusive at best."

At that, he turned back to his software and removed a video camera from a computer bag to record the event that had taken place on the door and floor but was shocked to find no remnants of the phenomena. Richard called to Will, and they looked everywhere for any shred of the ectoplasm that had vanished just as quickly as it had appeared.

"Well, at least we don't have to explain the mess," said Richard enthusiastically.

Will nodded. They both knew that he had taken pictures, and though unable to videotape the occurrence, they still had hard evidence on infrared film. It was still disputable, and many experts will claim flaws in the photograph, but to Richard, it was completely genuine. With today's technology, it is easy to tamper and alter photographic and video media, leaving a huge grey area for argument.

Will turned and slumped in the chair at the desk and opened his journal while pulling a pen from his pocket. He began writing down the times and occurrences of the day, giving thorough attention to that night. Then he handed the pen to Richard to record his experience while he rose and unstopped his bottle of scotch. He offered his brother a drink, and Richard gladly accepted the bottle for a swig.

Richard was tired, and it quickly consumed his excitement, turning him drowsy. The victory drinks also seemed to influence his brother, further hindering Will's state, and soon sleep overcame them.

CHAPTER FIVE

GHOSTS

Richard sat up. He was slumped over in one of the wing-backed chairs as Lucy swung open the heavy wooden door and entered the bedroom, pausing for a moment to glance at the computers on the floor. Will was sprawled over his desk with a half-empty bottle of scotch. Richard did not care to be seen, as they were still dressed in their clothes from the night before, and he was a little taken aback by her abruptness.

"You could have knocked first," he said with a smile, trying to be polite though his facial featues and eyes screamed for her to get out as she began to strip the bed of its sheets.

"I did, Mr. Stilton, many times. You have missed breakfast. It is early noon. Lunch will be served shortly, and I cannot wait for you to rise to finish my duties."

Will stirred and sat up in time to watch the ill-tempered Lucy close the door behind her. Her voice was soft, but her tone was scolding. He looked at Richard, who turned his gaze to him then back to the bed. "Breakfast?" queried Will.

"Lunch time," returned Richard with a smile.

"No, breakfast?" Will held up the bottle of scotch. Rays of sunlight refracted and broke through the auburn nectar.

"Breakfast!" replied Richard, his smile widening as he reached for the bottle. Investigations with his brother were always an adventure of their own. When they did happen, he enjoyed them immensely. It gave him a chance to delve into Will's world.

Lunch was stacked deli sandwiches served with select salads. Will and Richard had a chance to eat heartily before Mrs. Law entered the room. Richard took pleasure watching her: her demeanour, that regal air about her, the stench of old money. Her hair was pulled back, and two rows of braids encircled the crown of her head while the rest of her hair flowed down the back of her neck, ending between her shoulder blades. It was silver with streaks of brown. Her dress was form-fitting which accentuated her slight form, open enough to reveal her traps and clavicle before wrapping about her shoulders. This must have been a dress for pleasure, not business and he couldn't help but wonder how many years it had been since she ventured off the estate.

Mrs. Law's eyes gravitated to him, then looked away again. Her way of acknowledging his presence, he presumed. She stopped at the head of the table, Lucy pulled back the chair, and Mrs. Law sat down, her hands crossed, waiting for Lucy to finish doctoring up her coffee. She took a sip, her eyes not wavering, always on him.

"The other Mr. Stilton, I presume," she said tartly.

Richard smiled. "Yes, ma'am," he said, then took a sip of his coffee. He wasn't about to be intimidated, despite how impressive and grand she was, along with all of her estate. Richard watched as she paused for a moment. She was obviously impressed that he chose to acknowledge her with "ma'am," yet unimpressed he had. She continued nonetheless.

"Mrs. Law will suffice, Mr. Stilton."

Richard smiled and nodded his head in acknowledgement. "Yes, ma'am," he said politely, breaking eye contact as he reached for his coffee. Mrs. Law turned to Will, but he could feel Lucy glaring at him.

Richard listened as Will presented their findings thus far. He was confident and professional despite her lack of expression. Even Lucy stood behind her, cold as stone.

Will paused. With a glance to Richard, he mentioned without detail the events from the previous night and noted they were sending out the photographs to be developed.

Mrs. Law held up her hand in a gesture of silence, and Will's voice hushed. Her voice became abrasive at the mention of the phenomena on the door. Sternly, she reminded the two brothers they were there to prove any paranormal existence, not to disfigure her property. She leaned in, glaring with passionate anger, scolding the superstitions of her workers and the impact it was obviously having on her empire.

"Bring me results, Mr. Stilton, not stories. Prove to me there is actually something here. Right now, I don't see any evidence to suggest that, and I remain correct believing my workers' claims are unfounded," was her closing statement as she abruptly exited the room, leaving the two looking at one another.

"That was rough!" blurted Richard as he reached for another sandwich. He suggested mailing out the film to be developed, or they could go into town and pay out of their pockets to have the film developed for more immediate results. "It will get us out of the house for a time," he said as he finished his sandwich.

Will smiled. "Sure. It will be nice to get off the estate for a time and out of the musty house."

"Agreed. And we can ask locals about any rumours or lore on the house and property," Richard added with a heaping gulp of orange juice.

Will went back to his room to retrieve the film. He would meet Richard down at the van. The event from the previous night lingered on his mind. He knew what it was, but in his mind, in his processes, he had to exhaust all logical explanations before he could accept the idea that he and his brother were witnesses to paranormal phenomena. It was an arduous process, but it kept him grounded and firm in the investigation.

Will smiled as he jotted quickly in his journal. They could have something genuine. He lifted the camera from the writing desk and noticed there were four exposures remaining. Will sighed. He hated wasting film, but he really wanted to develop the photographs. As he fit his head and arm into the sling on the camera, so it slung across his chest, his gaze turned to the window.

Will paused and, with a smile, reached for the near-empty bottle of scotch, hoisted it to his lips and stopped. His eyes looked beyond the bottle out the window at the water fountain, where he noticed the very pretty gardener. He lowered the bottle from his mouth and placed it heavily on the table top.

Saraphima knelt at the fountain's edge, working in the surrounding garden and tending to her lilies, seemingly unaware that she was being watched. Behind her, large stone and formed concrete planters burst vibrantly with beautiful flowers. Ivy and hostas dotted the flagstone pathway among the cedar hedgerows that made up the labyrinth that was the bulk of the garden. He watched the beautiful gardener work her hands in the dirt and water. A long shirt that was done up to her neck and fitted about her torso accentuating her bust. It had dirt stains on the elbows. She wore overalls, the straps neatly fitting over her shoulders. Rolled cuffs ended at the ankles. It was a tapestry of dirty hand smudges and stained knees.

Will looked on with a modicum of adoration for a moment. He had really enjoyed their meeting previously and hoped to meet up with her again.

As Will drove the van through the old town, he noticed its character was ancient and solemn as it stood alone just outside the giant old growth forest that separated it from the Law estate and, apparently, the rest of the world. "Brackenstone" was displayed on the sign carved in a massive rocky outcrop covered in a black moss or lichen within the town's borders. Massive spruces and pines mixed with oaks and birches smothered the borders, opening up into a grassy plain with rocky outcrops jutting from the ground. The air about the community seemed dreary, yet the life of the locals was bustling as they went about their businesses and errands.

Will was conscious of how their van stood out. It was much more modern than the vehicles manoeuvring about the streets and therefore captured much attention as they entered the town. After they had found a parking spot, a small crowd of people gathered about to study the vehicle but kept their distance.

"I feel strange. People are watching us," Will muttered as he and Richard ventured into a photography store. The proprietor stood behind her counter, sizing them up as they approached her, clearly not quite sure what to make of the new duo in town, but she greeted them with a smile all the same. Richard presented her with the film, and she stated with confidence that she could have it ready for the following morning. Will would have preferred to have it ready before they ventured back to the estate but he was content to have it for the following day. It would be good to have something physical to bring with him to the next meeting with Mrs. Law, even if the photographs yielded little orbs that could just as easily be written off as dust or moisture in the air or on the lens. Still, it would be something.

If this was their idea of hasty, he'd hate to see their idea of slow. Every time he'd had film developed, there was a modicum of hope that perhaps they caught something on film, but he'd always kept it to himself. He thought for a brief moment of that time he'd captured the figure of a deceased housekeeper in an old grand house that belong to a wealthy railroad baron from the early nineteen-hundreds. When he had shown it to the owners of the house, now a bed and breakfast, they stated it must have been Nelly. She lived and died on the grounds and was still seen from time to time. She was his first photograph of a full-torso spectre in her period clothing.

The air in the streets was moist and smelled like rain, and a dampness clung to the buildings. The streets and walkways were well-kept, adorned with older street lamps and signs jutting from the front of businesses. Old wood splitting, years of paint cracking, and old sturdy brick walls displayed the town's age once again.

They came to a pub where Will ushered his brother in for a pint and, with hope, a hardy meal before heading back to the estate. The bartender, a man who looked as though he had seen and heard it all, happily obliged the duo with a couple of pints and a table for a meal. They sat and sipped their brews, taking in the sweet nectar of their stouts. In minutes, their meals came: a roast beef for Will and a leg of lamb for Richard. They gladly thanked the waitress and happily delved into their meals, quiet at first, but neither one could keep quiet about the previous night. They chatted excitedly as they devoured their meals, oblivious of the attention they were gathering.

"How is everything?" came the soft-voiced query, and the two brothers shifted their attention from the conversation to the nice young waitress standing at their table.

Richard happily ordered two more pints, but Will's attention was taken elsewhere. He leaned past the attendant, noticing that the room, once full of voices, had dwindled down to a few robust conversations. Eyes were on them. Some moved quickly away as his gaze met theirs, but others merely stared at them, paying no heed to his sudden agitation. He leaned back, giving the waitress a friendly smile. He could see on her face the embarrassment she was suffering from being the centre of attention as she moved to and from the newcomers in town.

With a smile in return, she turned and manoeuvred to the bar, leaving their table to reveal a man glaring at them, standing in the middle of the room. He was an older man dressed very English, in a weathered, long leather coat, a scarf wrapped loosely around his neck with a flat hat and a baggy sweater that hung below his trousers. He was on a mission; that is what his eyes revealed as he slowly made his way to the table. It was evident in his stride that he had been drinking. But to their misfortune, not enough to keep him at bay. As he approached, the man grasped a chair and pulled it to the table.

Will leaned back, crossing his arms as a barrier to the newcomer. Once before, he had been run out of a small-town hotel because of his interest and career, and it started very much like this moment was turning into. Richard had no reaction and didn't shift his body as Will had. Will knew his brother well enough to understand he was standing his ground, boldly waiting to see what this drunk had to say.

Before he sat down, he looked at the barkeep and with a simple gesture, a seemingly universal bar language, had a pint brought to the table he now made his home with the brothers.

"Pete," he said aloud before sitting down, keeping his eyes on Richard. "My name is Pete," he said, turning his attention to Will who hesitated to say anything.

"Yous two able to talk? Or Old Lady Law have your tongues cut." He leaned in on his left forearm as his right grasped the freshly delivered pint brought with Will and Richard's. He took a gulp and set it down, looking hard at the duo again. "Right," he muttered. "It's no secret the two of yous is stay'n at the Law estate back in the woods."

Will shot Richard a brief glance, eyebrow raised.

The man took another sip. "It also ain't any secret why you're there."

"Why are we here?" asked Richard, reaching for his brew.

Pete looked at him stunned. "Whadya mean why? Ya don't know?" he turned to Will. "Your friend looks smart, at least."

Will smiled at the comment and looked at Richard, who displayed an air of annoyance.

"Tell me, how can ya be somewhere and not know why? You some degree of lost?"

"Why do you think we are here," said Richard agitated.

Pete sat upright for a second. "Don't get yer knickers in a knot, friend." And then he leaned in again, gesturing for the two of them to lean in with him. "Ghosts," he whispered.

"Ghosts?" repeated Richard.

"What are ya? A fucking echo too!"

Will guffawed and then leaned in with the older man, grasping a hold of his pint too, in very much the same manner, and looking sternly at the man's hard expression.

"How did you come by this?" Richard was leaning in.

"By word of the workers on Mrs. Law's estate," he said in a low tone, looking around as if for any stray ears that should not be listening. "I worked on her estate for a time as an onsite carpenter. The workers talk, many of them come back to town daily. Word gets around pretty quick."

"Splendid," said Will as he leaned back in his chair, unimpressed with the news.

"What else have you heard?" asked Richard as he took a gulp of his beer.

"Of yous two? That's it. If I knew about the two of yous, you think I'd be sitt'n here talking to yas?"

Richard sighed.

"Rumours of the Law's." Pete's face lit up like a little boy, and he leaned in closer. "They say the old lady's cracked upstairs." He pressed his index finger to his temple, his eyes moving from Will to Richard as he spoke. "Stories of the late Mr. Law were that the ol' chap was have'n an affair with a lassie work'n on the estate. They say that when his ol' lady found out bout what her solicitous husband was up to, she developed an unwholesome personality."

Will was suddenly interested to hear more since he already had an uncouth opinion of Mrs. Law "What do you mean, 'unwholesome'?"

Pete was more enchanted by the sound of his own voice than the two and was more than happy to regale them with stories of his former employer whom he seemed to have a disgust for.

"Well, firstly, she was dress'n more and more elaborate all the time, as though she were go'n to some big ball but wandered the grounds as if her prince charm'n had never showed. They say she was try'n to get her husband's undivided attention but it wasn't work'n. But, lots of the boys noticed him every morn'n kiss'n a lady, appear'n to be her, but some of the boys told tales of an affair with one of the maids. Kiss'n her on the neck on their balcony overlook'n the vineyard. They'll tell yas, there was true love in that ol' man's heart fer her, whoever she was."

He paused to take a heaping gulp from his pint. Wiping the foam from his lips, he started again as if he were telling a campfire legend. "Then I noticed her revolution. She was starin' at the girls with wickedness in her eyes. It'd take a fool not to notice the hatred she had for them. There were some that she liked..."

"Lucy?" said Will.

"A vile lass," he quickly rebutted at the very mention of the name. "But aye, Lucy was her favourite girl. Ever faithful Lucy. That woman did what she could to stay in Mrs. Law's favour, almost as though she had somteth'n to prove... so I heard." He took a drink from his pint and wiped the foam from his beard.

"Mrs. Law wasn't certain which one of the girls had won her husband over, so the spiteful ol' woman took her hatred out on those she saw with her husband or those who she figured enchanted her man. Story goes, Lucy spied on Mrs. Law's husband and on the other lasses that worked the estate, when she wasn't stand'n by Mrs. Law's side."

Richard drained the last of his pint then looked up from the bottom of his glass. " Mrs. Law didn't seek sexual relations with any of the men working on the estate?"

Pete looked at him with wickedness in his eyes. "Not a one. Some gents tried, but their employ, I can tell ya, it didn't last long… some time after she expected the girls to be enchant'n her dearest, some went miss'n. Word at first was that she fired them but then stories began to leak from the forsak'n walls of the house. Talk of ghosts and hauntings stirred in the ears and minds of the workers… they say the ol' lady killed many of the lasses after axe'n her own husband. He hadn't been seen long before rumours started. Never even saw a funeral in procession, though some would be inclined to disagree. Consider this your warn'n, friends. Leave that place as I did. Don't look back an' go home." He finished his pint and then stood. With a tip of his hat, he turned and made for the door.

Will looked at Richard, who was still watching the carpenter hobble off. Then Richard called out, "Pete. Hey Pete!"

He turned and set his eyes on the duo at the table.

"Have you ever seen anything?"

He stood for a second, and his gaze drifted to the floor for but a second that felt like a diminutive eternity. Then it snapped back up to Richard with a fleeting disconcert. "Naw," he said gruffly, shaking his head. He then turned and vanished into the diminishing daylight beyond the door.

CHAPTER SIX

SILENT SCREAMS

Will listened to Richard chatting excitedly as he drove back to the estate. He was bubbling over about what the new night may yield, what potential phenomena may be deemed paranormal, and the validity of Pete's story in the pub.

"He seemed to know the estate and the lore behind Mrs. Law, but the problem with stories and rumours is they are mutable, always taking on new twists and turns as they are regaled from one person to another," said Will, turning his gaze out the side window. He watched the darkening world pass by with all its long shadows reaching from the forest to the van with long grim fingers.

"And soon you have the evolution of a rumour continually budding," agreed Richard, who kept his eyes on the road ahead, the last rays of sunlight stretching over the treetops and reflecting off his sun glasses.

As they neared the top of the long driveway, they were greeted by Lucy standing on the front step of the giant mansion with a bland expression on her face—a reflection of her personality. Yet again, Richard greeted her with a smile, and his endearing humor was all in vain as she shrugged him off with little grace.

Will watched as she did so and shook his head as Richard turned to him, smiling, clearly unfazed by the grim personality of the lady. Lucy appeared to be pleased to inform the two that Mrs. Law would not be joining them for dinner that evening nor for breakfast in the morning to follow, but she still expected a full report of their progress thus far. At that, she turned and marched through the large doors.

"I hope you're not trying to get on her good side… if she has one," muttered Will to Richard as he watched her disappear.

The tall, dark man gave him a grimace at the very thought of the two of them bonding.

"Hell, no!" He nearly bawled. "Being nice is the one thing I don't believe she can tolerate, or at least handle much of," he countered with a vile smirk on his lips.

Will smiled as he went into the building with his brother following.

The night was a rerun of the previous; once again, Will manoeuvred the corridors and open rooms of the house while Richard planted himself in the room. Once again, everything seemed quiet. They chatted amongst themselves serenely, keeping open communication with one another and helping to calm each other's nerves. It was a rule of thumb and always important to go on investigations in a team rather than take on the paranormal world by one's self. Having company helps to keep a clear head and maintain focus on the job; added perspectives are always a bonus.

Will ambled down the corridor to and fro, testing door knobs and handles. Those that opened, he ventured in, exploring the room and the atmosphere. It was usually drab, with very little signs of traffic ever moving in or out. The expectation for something to happen was even greater now, for both the brothers. They had become anxious as the night progressed and oversensitive to their surrounding environments. The slightest transferences set them on their toes, rushing animatedly to investigate, but with the calmness of the night thus far, their enthusiasm had dwindled.

Richard sat up from his cozy spot on the floor where his computer equipment lay strewn about and started for the chair at the writing desk; a warm thermos of caffeinated brew rested beside Will's favoured bottle of depleting scotch. After unscrewing the top, he poured himself a mugful then turned his gaze to the bottle. There wasn't much. He would tap into the new bottle his brother had bought earlier that day and flavour his otherwise insipid coffee.

He came back to the desk, removing the cork cap with a *thupe*. A half a shot would do; he figured he could always add more if he had to. Richard couldn't see his brother being upset with him for delving into the new bottle already. If anything, he should be proud of him embracing it. Hoisting the mug to his mouth, he took a generous sip of the flavoured coffee, savouring the taste of caffeinated scotch warming his chest as it made its way down. Another sip was in order, but the coffee missed his mouth completely, and a small morsel fell onto his collar and chest.

He reacted accordingly, pulling back from the mug; his jaw dropped and his eyes wide as he glared out the window. He set the mug down and leaned over the desk, ignoring the sharp burning sensations lingering from the coffee. His heart began to race, his breathing quickened, and his body temperature started to rise with the trauma of what he was witnessing. A woman leaned over, no, suspended off the rocks as her torso bobbed face down in the water of the fountain. Her long blonde hair spread from her head in clumps, undulating with the water as it stirred. Her dress, saturated and fanned out, floated on the surface, the tips of her black dress shoes just barely touching the ground, scuffing on the dirt as the fountain upset her lifeless body.

Will stumbled, nearly falling to the floor as he ripped the headset from his ear, Richard's voice thundering on the other end. After retrieving the communication device, Will called back to his brother, who was still rambling on.

"A woman? Wha...what woman? Rich... Richard! What?" he responded as calmly as he could. He could hear his brother's heavy breaths heaving into the microphone, and his footfalls as he scrambled through the house. "The wha... the fountain!"

He had heard enough; he knew where Richard was going. He rushed out of the room he was in, barely registering the sound of the legs on the old wood chair sliding across the dusty floor above the voice in his earpiece.

Richard pushed open the large, heavy doors that strained his shoulders with their resistance as he forced the two at once. Spilling himself into the midnight air, he felt its damp coolness refreshing. It exhilarated him further as he scuttled down the stairs into the gardens. Behind him, he heard the rush of running feet, and a shoulder check revealed Will was mere moments behind him, forcing himself through the closing doors and catching up to where he stood yards from the fountain. Its waters trickled and rippled with its own currents. Tiny waves caught the moonlight, distorting its mirror image on the cold water as it fluidly fell from one level of the fountain to the next. Richard stood in disbelief. His breathing was heavy, and he sensed Will's eyes on him.

"Why so frantic? What's going on?" Will asked.

"She was right there," he said, pointing a quivering finger at the base of the fountain closest to them.

"Who was there, Richard?" Will answered sternly as he manoeuvred to stand in front of him, cutting off his view of the fountain and catching his gaze.

Richard paused for a moment, seeing his brother, then relaxed a bit as a calming fell over him.

"I have to admit, bro, for a big guy, I have never seen you like this," said Will as he placed a hand on one of Richard's arms, giving it a firm squeeze.

Richard smiled in return and leaned slightly to look over Will's shoulder at the fountain once more. His breathing slowed as he regained his composure then ushered his brother aside. He made his way to the falling water and sat on the edge of the stone. "It was here, exactly where I am sitting. There was a woman lying face down in the water."

He placed his hand to the stone; it was surprisingly warm to the touch. He had expected something much colder like the glider rocker in their room. He had not mentioned it to Will yet, and he was unsure if he should, especially now. Everything felt so surreal after the incident with the door.

"She appeared to be wearing an older Victorian-style dress." Richard paused and thought for a moment. "Something similar to what that Broom woman wears."

Will smiled. "You mean your girlfriend?"

Richard glared at him, unimpressed. "She is not my girlfriend, so stop it."

Will laughed. "I don't know; I have felt some kind of energy between you two."

Richard shook his head. "Are you done?"

Will nodded, still chuckling to himself.

"Anyways, she looked so real! The way she laid in the water. I swear, man, if that was not a woman, and not some kind of repeating phantasm, then I don't know what it was, and quite frankly, it's kind of creepy."

"This whole place is creepy, bro," agreed Will, his eyes manoeuvering over the grounds as if expecting something else to happen.

They ventured back to their room, where Richard thought it best they view the camera data before starting anew if they made it that far. As they examined the video, they found nothing out of the ordinary.

"Richard, I think it's appropriate that I explain something," said Will, turning to his brother. "When I was talking to Saraphima, there was a girl sitting on the edge of the fountain, watching. She did not acknowledge that girl, not once in the time I saw her. She wore the same garments you describe, bro."

Richard just sat looking at Will, expressionless. "This could be the real deal, Will! We could be in the midst of some real paranormal activity! By far the biggest investigation we have ever had!… or at least the most authentic and revealing."

Will sat down in his chair at the desk, poured himself a scotch, and leaned back. "Problem is, Old Lady Law doesn't even acknowledge the existence of ghosts, apparitions, spectres, or any other phenomena, for that matter. She refuses to listen to her workers who are scared of something and are constantly refusing work… or leaving. To scare off one worker is one thing, but to frighten a whole estate is something else entirely." He took a sip of scotch. "I'm not saying the place is genuinely haunted, yet, despite what we've seen, there is something unsettling about the Law estate."

Richard nodded. "I look forward to seeing the photographs tomorrow. I am hoping they reveal something we have not yet seen or possibly overlooked."

Will set his glass down. "I took a picture of the girl sitting on the fountain."

His brother sat up from his laptop, which was still lying on the floor. "I equally anticipate the pictures!"

Will threw back the last of the scotch in his glass and stood up, donning the headset once again.

"Are you online? Do you have eyes?" Richard looked at his monitor, and with a wisp of his hands and the clacking of a keyboard, he nodded with a smile.

Will exited the room, and Richard picked up his video transmission on the monitor, watching as he made his way down the hall to where he had left off, checking door knobs as he went. The image brightened as Will came to the sconces that now burned brightly where before they flickered aggressively. He saw Will place his hand to them.

"Wow, these are really warm. They seem to be putting out too much heat, as far as I'm concerned. The EMF meter is slightly elevated, too. Could be due to the lights and the old wires running through the walls."

Richard monitored his computers vigilantly, flipping screens to view in colour or infrared, stopping frames and moving them to another screen to view small details such as things moving in the background, figures, and shadows. So far, it was boring. He took it very seriously, straining every panel, dissecting it with his eyes, but so far, he had come up with nothing. Everything was ordinary, but the incident with the fountain continuously played back in his mind. It was so fresh and unexplainable. He was still on edge, always wanting to peek out the window to see if she were there once more. Is she? What would he do?!

His eyes slowly trained themselves on the window, away from the computers for a moment, knowing full well he could miss something. But what was he missing out there?

Should he venture a look? He looked back at the screens. Will was making his way into a ballroom. Neither one of them was acquainted with ballrooms, so as his brother paused to survey the grand beauty of the room, Richard looked on in wonder through his computer screen. Beautiful polished floors, a slew of round tables shrouded by their decorative tablecloths and surrounded by chairs. Each table with its respective chairs was spaced evenly throughout the room, making it appear larger than it was. Fine wood carvings in each corner accented the crown moulding and the walls were adorned with a wallpaper that appeared to be laced with gold and silver and embellished with red stripes that reached from the fourteen-inch baseboards up towards the ceiling.

Richard slowly stood, ever keeping his eyes on the screens, as he backed toward the desk just before the window. His palms touched the chair's back, bringing his body to a halt. His nerves were frantic. What could be behind him? Only a pane of glass separated him from what he witnessed, and it really wasn't comforting. Should he?

"Ah, shit!" he blurted to himself. "I came this far. Man up, Richard." And with his newfound strength, he turned to the window.

There was nothing there. The fountain stood alone. Richard's eyes manoeuvred over the gardens, but nothing was there. He breathed a sigh of relief; he wanted to see something, but he was satisfied with nothing as the night had already yielded plenty to him. He was content. He sat back down at his computers and played a melody on his keyboard, solely fixed on Will as a vague shadow crept over the wall.

Will cautiously manoeuvred around the table in the ballroom; its appearance was fresh as if it were just set, but it also suggested that it had not been formerly utilized in many years. The room was big and his footfalls, as minute as they were, sent soft echoes reverberating throughout.

He glanced at his EMF meter. It was reading 0.03 kilojoules (kJ) which was about average, considering his body put out its own magnetic field.

Will pulled a chair out from its resting spot with a heavy grinding of wood on wood and sat down. "This may be a nice spot for some EVRs."

But there was no reply from his brother's end. He paused for a moment and leaned forward. "Richard. Richard, are you there?" He tapped his earpiece. Suddenly, the chair beside him slid out from the table, grinding on the floor as it was forced across the room. Then, like some undulating beast, all the chairs in the room started moving, shuffling about their tables, all grinding at the floor pugnaciously with him at the centre.

Will, stunned for a moment by the sudden activity, came back to his senses as a chair was hurled over a table, striking him in the side, causing him to falter, and he fell to one knee. Will lifted his arms to protect his head as another chair slid across the floor, striking him in the shoulder. Will pulled himself to his feet amidst the chaos. The sounds of the multitude of chairs gliding across the floor were almost deafening. Another chair came at him, but he dodged it as he ran to the door. Frantically he grabbed his earpiece. "*Richard!*"

Richard stumbled backwards, his body saturated. Water ran from his hair and his sleeves to the floor as though he were standing in a torrential downpour. The glider rocker rocked fiercely before him, and shadows reached from the corners of the room like long menacing tendrils as water dripped from the walls and pooled on the floor around him. He grabbed at his shirt and pulled it open around the collar, ever aware of the menacing glider rocker. His breathing was laboured and grew shallow; he could not draw any more air into his lungs.

Richard fell to the floor, struggling to breathe. He was coughing and hacking and then gargling and choking as water started to pour from his mouth to the floor. His eyes widened, filling with fear, and he grabbed at his chest and throat. He rolled onto his back as water continued to bubble and flow from his mouth, down the side of his face to the floor. He shivered with cold as the smell of the fountain outside surrounded him while the air about him turned hot and humid.

Just then, Will burst into the room with a grunt. "Richard!"

Richard felt him fall to his side as he hacked and wheezed on the floor, water trickling and drooling from his lips and spraying from his mouth. He slowly regained his breathing, drawing in deeply.

Will picked him up to his knees, Richard's chin resting on his shoulder. "Good God! You're soaked! What happened to you!?"

It took a moment for Richard to reply; his body was slouched over as he lifted his head to look his brother in the eyes. "I… I don't… know."

Lucy came frantically to the door donning her nightgown, her brown hair loose, hanging over her shoulders to her bosom. Strands of grey were far more visible now. "I demand to know what you are doing! You… What happened to him?" She entered the room and looked over Will's shoulder at the slouched, soaking wet man.

"Please, come on in," muttered Will as he wrestled Richard to the bed and sat him down. "You're sleeping here tonight, bro."

Richard nodded, watching as Will turned, walked to the table where the scotch stood, took a swig, and then pulled the bottle from his lips in disgust. "What the hell! This is watered right down!"

"Have you been drinking? Is that what all this is about?" queried Lucy in a stern tone.

Will placed the bottle back on the table and glared at her for a moment with the same judging expression. "No, my dear. We have not."

Richard stood, a little shaken but steadily regained his composure. He started to remove certain articles of clothing which fell with a *slop* to the floor, keeping an ever-vigilant eye on the glider rocker that now sat quietly.

"What happened in the ballroom, Mr. Stilton?"

Will just looked at her.

"All the chairs are piled up! In the middle of the room! And you have not the slightest explanation why?"

Will turned, walked up to her, and stood mere inches from her face. "You wouldn't believe me even if I told you. You brought us here for reasons we thought we knew. I cannot explain away what happened in that room, nor here, which leads me to ponder the notion that there is something here that you know about, that you refuse to talk to us about and refuse to acknowledge, and we will find out what it is."

"No, Mr. Stilton. It looks to me as though you had been drinking too much and concocted your own ghosts." At that, she turned to walk out the door, but Will grasped her arm. She turned with a cold, hard look of anger.

"What is going on here, Lucy?"

She wrenched her arm from his grasp and stormed down the hallway, disappearing into the shadows of the night.

Richard, now regaining his composure, held up the bottle of scotch that was now diluted with water. Undaunted, he took a swig and placed it down, debating on a second sip but corked it instead. He turned his attention to the glider rocker, no longer rocking menacingly but standing still. Richard hesitantly placed his hand on the chair. Its fabric was warm to the touch.

Will Started hefting the electronic hardware onto the bed, turning it over, one by one. "Hmm, I don't think any water got in. It all seems sound." He mumbled small curses and threats at their hosts in slight disgust and at himself for taking the job. He stormed over to the bottle of scotch, where he took a large gulp, grimacing in frustration at its diluted state again, but it was better than nothing.

"This is going to go over well tomorrow, don't you think?" uttered Richard as he crawled into bed, exhaustion making his body heavy.

"Piss on them," scorned Will as he sat in the chair. Water shot from the cushion and dripped to the floor. He rubbed his eyes, very aware of the saturated chair and not caring.

CHAPTER SEVEN

THE PHOTOGRAPH

The following morning, Will was quite relieved that Mrs. Law would be unable to meet with them for breakfast but sent instructions for them to carry out their duties without further obstruction. This made their breakfast quiet and very enjoyable. Lucy took the time to inform them that they could not use the telephone, but instead, they could go into town to see if their pictures were developed. Will suspected she took a great deal of pleasure in denying them a convenience, but Richard seemed unfazed by the unruly gesture and confessed he could stand for a pint.

Later that morning, Will and Richard took to the orchard to speak with some of the workers. To their knowledge, they had evaded Lucy and her insufferable gaze that kept constant tabs on them. The workers were not as willing to speak as they had hoped, keeping their attention only to their task, alienating the two investigators to the point of frustration. It was then they heard someone calling; a lone worker waved them away from the rest. They followed him out of the orchard and into the vineyard away from the workers.

Richard was more concerned than Will as the foreman pleaded for them to leave, proving that the workers were useless for any kind of data-gathering. The two headed back to the house.

"The workers come off just as superstitious as Mrs. Law had mentioned, if not more so," said Richard, looking over his shoulder to see if the foreman were still watching them depart.

"Which can reduce a case's legitimacy, unfortunately. I wonder if Ol' Lady Law knew this?"

"Agreed," replied Will. "Superstition on this level and under the right circumstances could lead to, in this case, mass paranoia. Talking about it, or acknowledging the presence of a paranormal entity in any way, can give it power."

Richard nodded. "They really are in a pickle. On the one hand, they dread coming to work, and on the other hand, they need to provide for their families." Will looked up at his brother with a slight grin. "There is fuckary afoot, Watson."

Will kept a vigil out for Saraphima. It had been days since he had seen her last.

Richard smiled. "Other than myself, I believe she is the only person you take pleasure in seeing."

Will looked ahead, then to his brother. "There is a shortage of good things in this world, bro."

They had decided: Richard would go to town for the photograph while Will stalked about the grounds looking for anything that may help aid them. Secretly, Will was hoping to run into the cute gardener again, and his brother called him on it. They parted at the stone steps out front of the heavy doors of the estate.

Richard looked up to see where they were, yet still, under the watchful gaze of Lucy, who was peering from one of the open windows of Mrs. Law's office.

"Speak of the devil!" he said out loud.

"And she will appear!" continued Will as, he too, turned and looked up. They both had foolish grins.

"I have been tasked with keeping an eye on the both of you, Messrs. Stilton," responded Lucy. She was glaring at the two.

"So we've noticed," replied Will as his brother turned and climbed into the company van.

As Richard pulled away, he glanced up and gave the grave woman a wink.

Will watched his brother pull away then went about his business.

I should wait for Richard to check out that family cemetery, Will thought to himself. *But I hate waiting. Perhaps I can get a camera set up in there before Rich gets back.* Will nodded to himself, satisfied with his decision. This wasn't the first estate he had been hired to investigate, but so far, it had proven to be the strangest. More compelling phenomena had occurred around him and his bro than at any other place. Most owners are begging for them to find something and some are disappointed while others are relieved, but this hag? Shit, she doesn't even want to know, and what they bring to her table, she dismisses. "Bitch," he said as he manoeuvred through the gardens.

"Excuse me!" came a familiar voice.

Will looked up and just a few yards from him, among tangled flowers and low cedar branches, was Saraphima looking at him with her pleasant eyes, her face adorned with a warm smile. Will's face flushed as he stopped in his tracks.

"Oh, sorry. Not you. I was thinking of someone else. She has been giving me a rough go."

The young woman chuckled to herself and emerged from the trees and flowers. Her knees and shins on her coveralls were filthy, and her hands were darkened with soil. "So, Mr. Stilton," she said in a playful tone, "what are you looking for?"

Will smiled. "I'm looking for some key areas to place some cameras and perhaps venture to the family cemetery."

"So, pretty much anything of interest that will aid you on your hunt." She looked at him in a way that could easily be perceived as flirting. A surge of allurement rushed through Will. He was becoming quite smitten with Saraphima.

"Tell me, Mr. Will. You are the hunter. Shouldn't a hunter know his quarry?"

He was taking great pleasure in this. "I have to be sceptical. If I believe everything, then I'll see anything. The more I cannot disprove, the more I will prove."

"I see," she exclaimed. "Well, my deist friend, beyond this garden, near the courtyard and a grove of oaks, is my house.

It was getting late. Richard was at the local pub having a pint before heading back to the estate. Sipping his nectar, he slowly sifted through the photographs one by one, pulling them closer then holding them out as he carefully studied each picture. Reaching for his pint once again, he froze, disregarding the rest of the photos save one. His eyes widened. Releasing his pint, he grasped the picture with two hands to steady himself. It was of the fountain below their window, where he had sworn he had seen a woman in the water.

"There you are, my dear," he said to himself, slowly raising the glass to his lips then wiping away the froth. There she was indeed, clear as day: the young woman floating in the fountain. A bit of sadness befell him at that moment. His body became heavy, then he felt soft hands rest on his shoulders.

Richard turned, but there was no one around save the patrons at their own tables, paying him no heed. Quickly, he paid his tab and rushed out, eager to show Will the photograph and pondering what Mrs. Law would say.

Shadows began to stretch across the roads and walkways, and street lamps sang their *hum* as the sun was setting and the darkness settled. The sky was dominated by a half-moon and a plethora of stars. The road was winding in his headlights. No sign of anyone heading toward him nor in his follow; it was a lonesome drive. Tree tops became twisted, mangled figures peering down on him in the soft glow from above.

"*Shit!*" His eyes widened, and his body tensed. He brought the van to a screeching halt, veering away from the woman who had emerged from the forest.

Frantically stumbling, she held her arms out with open palms, mere feet from his vehicle; she seemed completely oblivious of him. Dirty and distraught, she wore a long, torn nightgown smeared with stains. She stumbled past the front of the vehicle, disappearing into the darkness once again.

Richard exited the van and called out to her. There was no response. Images of the woman in the fountain came to him as he replayed in his mind what just happened. He checked his phone, walking front to back, around the idling machine and back to the driver's door. No signal. Typical. Exasperated, he climbed back into the van, scanned the area one more time, then slipped the vehicle into gear. Lurching forward ever so slowly, it abruptly quit, the engine stalling out.

"What the hell," he muttered to himself, even more on edge now. Suddenly, his joints tightened, and his body ached and stiffened. Gripping the steering wheel with an unnatural strength, he was completely immobile. He groaned as he abruptly became aware of an agony he had never felt before coursing throughout him. It was torturous, and he felt helpless.

Hairs stood on end, and his skin became frigid. In the passenger seat sat the female, crouched and facing him. Her mouth was moving, the terror and agony showing. Hisses and gargling were all that emanated from her contracting throat. Harder and harder she tried to communicate, but only blood began to trickle from the corners of her once-beautiful lips.

Her eyes widened, and her face tensed in frustration as more blood spilled forth, now running down her chin, on her nightgown, and saturating the van seat. She started to creep across the seat, leaning into his ear then directly into his face. Her matted light-coloured hair brushed his cheek, and there was a foulness in the air. From her grotesque maw, blood splattered his face, shirt, and pants. A bloody, broken hand grasped the breast of his shirt, clawing into his chest. Stricken with utter fear, Richard squeezed his eyes shut.

"*Sss-ht-ee.*" The word, uttered in the most grotesque voice, suddenly resounded in his ear. He mustered a scream, a long, piercing shrill that seemed to drain the rest of his resilience. Then it was quiet. Richard opened his eyes. The van was empty, save him.

Will put the near-empty bottle to the rim of the glass for the third time. His patience was running thin. He left Saraphima's little cottage so he could finish installing the rest of the cameras around the garden before his brother returned. Fixed on the gateway, the camera remained dark, and there was no van in the drive.

"I could have put some in the family cemetery," he groaned. "Hitting my head off a brick wall would be better than this."

Then his thoughts trailed off to the locals from their previous visit to the town. They were not necessarily the nicest, welcoming bunch he had ever encountered, but the moment was a fleeting one. Richard was a robust, towering man, and he knew how to fight, despite his happy, charming demeanour. His thoughts drifted to Pete. His character, to Will, seemed like one who would spend his days in the drink at the local tavern. He then wondered what would happen if he had met Richard and tried to engage him, perhaps in playful bantering or regaling him in more lore regarding the Law estate. *Would Rich even give him the time?* he thought to himself, knowing his brother had an utter distaste for the drunkard. *What if it turned foul?*

Will smiled as he thought of the big man, Pete, trying to overpower his brother. His thoughts drifted to a time when three locals in Glasgow, Scotland, had a sudden beef with the big man. Will had wrestled one of the Scotsmen off Richard's back. They had only exchanged a few blows before Rich spun the man around and broke his jaw. The other two were sprawled out on the ground, undoubtedly with similar afflictions. He remembered looking up at that big smile with a shiner and a badly split lip. They never did find out what the issue was. *Nope, if Pete decided to poke the proverbial bear, he won't be doing shots at the bar. Richard would get them all in.* That brought a modicum of comfort to will as he took another sip of his drink.

Peering over the rim of his glass once again, Will saw that the trees and gateway became illuminated by the two headlights charging up the laneway. The van came to an abrupt halt at the base of the steps. Concern flushed over Will as the vehicle door flew open with Richard fumbling out. He was gawkish and ungainly as he made his way up the steps.

A *thud* resounded as Will slammed the glass to the table and made for the hallway. He marched, every bit of agitation and concern in his steps. Rounding a corner, he came to the long steps that ushered its occupants to the foyer. Racing down, he was abruptly confronted by the miserable-looking Lucy. At the base of the stairs, holding on to the banister, her body was rigid and her face expressionless save her eyes— they were judging as they seemed to always be.

Lucy stepped in, then stepped back, wincing.

"You have been indulging, Mr. Stilton? A pastime indicative of your poor character," she said harshly.

Will paused in thought for a second, a cold smirk developing. "Actually, Lucy, I ran out of liquor some time ago. All I could find was your bottle of bitch." He shot her a twisted smile.

"I am at a loss as to what Mrs. Law sees in you," was all she could muster.

Will was quick and ruthless. "That is it? I'm a little diss…"

Just then, the front door flew open, with Richard stumbling in. Sweating and dishevelled, his shirt was matted and hanging off him with a distorted blood stain on his chest.

"Holy shit!" Will thrust himself past Lucy, nearly knocking her down the small flight she had ascended. A grunt, followed by a plethora of curses, met his ears as she grasped the banister to keep from tumbling.

"What the hell happened to you?!"

Richard just looked at his brother; his expression was hard and intense. He took his time regaining his composure and brandished the developed photograph.

Will was dumbfounded. "Holy shit!" he said again. It was all he could think to say. It was uncommon to get a photograph with solid, irrefutable spectral phenomena, but in this instance, it was vital and powerful.

Despite his haggard condition, Richard mustered a chuckle. "I came in contact with one."

Will's expression did not change.

"Or, rather, she came into contact with me." He held out his shirt with the handprint on his chest and chuckled again.

"Fuck me!" Will added as he pulled the shirt open to get a better look at the hand print.

He heard Lucy gasp beside him.

The duo turned their attention to Lucy. Will held up the photograph of the woman in the fountain, and the two watched as her eyes widened in disbelief. "What are you not telling us? She is wearing the same dress as you. She is in your fountain."

Her eyes darted between the two brothers, then her expression hardened, and her voice was placid. "You have a photograph, Mr. Stilton. Good for you." With that, she marched up the stairs. "I will inform Mrs. Law." And she was gone.

"I can't wait to see how this plays out in the morning," exclaimed Richard, who was well enough to stand on his own, toying with the buttons on his shirt.

"Shut up," replied Will with a gesture upstairs. "C'mon, let's get you cleaned up."

The duo made their way upstairs to Richard's room.

"She truly is a bitch," growled Will as he followed his brother through the doorway. "And I thought I could be cold."

He studied Richard, who was methodically unbuttoning his shirt. He then took notice of Richard's satchel and was delighted at the colourful insignia that branded the bottle of scotch. Without hesitation, he pried the cork from the bottle and, with a hefty swig, made his way to his brother, whose shirt had been removed.

As red as it could be, a small hand seared onto his chest. Will looked closer, handing the bottle to Richard who didn't falter in bringing the bitter sweet liquid to his lips.

"Does it hurt?" posed Will as he probed around it gently.

"What the fuck do you think?" Richard glared at him cynically. "Remember that time we were in that small house up north?"

Will thought about it for a moment. "The one with the swinging chandelier?"

"Yeah. Remember when we were attacked by the entity, and we were scratched all to hell?"

Will laughed. "Yeah! I still blame you for that, but it was after that we knew we were dealing with a genuine paranormal force. We could stow away the scepticism and really buckle down."

"You mean you could stow away the scepticism," retorted Richard quickly, not willing to miss his chance. He knew that Will was a believer, and Will knew it too, but over the years of debunking cases, he became harder to convince and needed more and more proof.

Richard got comfortable, leaning back against the headboard, still running his hand around the mark on his chest. "You told me to instigate it! Anyways, it stings like that. It's not so bad I cannot function."

Will laughed. "Yeah, I did! One of the cases that had some real legitimacy to it."

Richard handed the bottle back to his brother. "Yeah, that priest never did get back to us."

Will pondered for a moment. "Not even a letter. Anyways, how are you feeling for later tonight?"

Richard thought briefly and nodded. "I want you to take a picture of this, but it would have been more legitimate if it was on video. This can be easily fabricated."

Will walked over to the satchel, pulled a small camera from it, and proceeded to take shots of the print. "This will be for our own records then."

It was nine o'clock, and the two decided they would get up at one o'clock to proceed with the night.

Will made his way back to his room, snatched up the glass he had been drinking from, and hastily strolled back to Richard's room. He hoped his brother hadn't fallen asleep yet and it would truly suck if he did. Will pushed open his brother's door with such force the hefty hinged barrier nearly extended its reach and creaked with a whisper.

"What the hell!" A startled Richard was sitting up, and his eyes were wide with excitement. "Don't you think I've been through enough tonight without you barging in on me?"

Will laughed his annoying victorious laugh. He needed to not explain himself. Richard, he was sure, already knew why he was there.

"For fuck sake, bro! You could have just taken the freaking bottle." He watched as Will poured a generous helping and placed the corked bottle back into his satchel.

"Nope!" he exclaimed. "We need this bottle to last. As much as I would love to embrace my one true love right here," he gestured to the scotch, "I will retain my reserve and only take what is needed and leave this beautiful concoction in your care." With that, he took his leave.

"I'm judging you right now," hollered Richard as the door whispered to a close.

Will pushed his way into his room, tasting the peaty nectar and reminiscing on the day. He was happy Richard was back and in as good of health as he could be, but he thought fondly of his time with the beautiful Saraphima. He paused with a smile and a modicum of sadness; it really was too bad they couldn't take her with them. His feeling of fondness was growing for the gardener and her wit. Another sip as he crawled under his sheets while cradling the drink and staring out the moonlit window. A slight glow enveloped his eyes and cheeks; their time here had not yet expired, and perhaps there was still hope for this hopeless man yet.

"What are you doing now, my dear," he uttered to himself as he gazed through the panes of glass and fell into slumber.

CHAPTER EIGHT

ELATION

Her hand touched his, gently grasping it. Her warm weight shifted on top of him, softly caressing his body. Warm breath brushed his chest as her hands caressed his arms up to the shoulders. Her beautiful hair, a cascading auburn waterfall, flowed across his pecs as she placed her ear to his breast. Her body shifted, and her pelvis pressed heavily against his as her lips gently cosseted his bosom, making their way to his clavicle.

Will nearly gasped and shuddered. She exhaled on his neck laboriously as her hands, which had a chill to them, grasped his biceps, holding his arms in place. A kiss of her lips, a touch of her tongue in the mid of his throat, as it explored the curvature of his jaw. Her nipples swayed, fluttering against his breast and ribs. Her lips pressed into his, so succulently soft and powerful, in an embrace that released emotions in him that had escaped him so many years ago. Will's body involuntarily relaxed, giving in to desire, a strong submission he had no conviction to fight, and he was overcome by exhilaration. His reaction was delayed. A tongue, velvety soft, touched his upper lip, and he opened his eyes to behold she that hovered over him. Her large eyes gazed back, piercing and striking. He was absolutely consumed. His being had been taken, and he possessed no desire to resist. His body was paralyzed from his mind. Her full weight came down on him, wrapping about him in an intimate embrace. He could feel the lack of warmth from her body as he fell under her influence.

She kissed him again, and it was as bewitching as it was exquisite. She was cool and wet as she gripped his body, slow and passionately rhythmic at first, not daring to break his gaze.

Their hands explored one another blindly for the first time, alternating between soft caressing and firm placing. He was taken as she leaned back in ecstasy with his hands upon her luscious breasts as she clutched his wrists. The muscles in her stomach and hips undulated as she pulled herself forward and pushed herself back.

He was abducted by the elation. Her breasts were cool and soft in his hands, her breathing became laboured, and her cold thighs tightened about him. Euphoric sighs escaped her lips as she exhaled into the air and onto his body. She pressed hard, pushing forcefully onto him. Her hands dug into his ribs as their bodies tightened in climactic ecstacy, and he was enamoured by the hot surge that flushed him, by her tensing muscles that bound his waist.

Will's heart fluttered as she leaned forward, draping her spent body over his own. Placing a finger over his lips to hush any words he might have, she gently leaned into his ear, speaking with a voice so melodious, "Wake up, William. Wake up."

Will suddenly shuddered to life. His heart was racing, his breathing was laborious, and his body was tacky. The scotch he had been pampering himself with had spilled all over his chest, save for a few sips. He sat up; his torso reeked of the liquor, but his waist and abdominals were saturated and clammy. He was covered in ejaculate.

The bed sheets were pushed from the mattress, and the room was astonishingly cold with the exception of where he lay. Bewildered, Will arose from the bed and moved to the bathroom where he ran a shower to clean up.

Will stood in the hot shower as though he were trying to regain his warmth. He could feel her as if she were still there, her body wrapped about his own. Emotions of anger, frustration, and self-pity surged through him. Flashes of the woman's face played and replayed through his mind as he let the hot water run down his body. Was he looking at Brynn? Tears fell from his eyes, caressing his cheeks and mixing with the hot water as everything he had suppressed came to the surface once again. For a moment, he was enveloped by a sense of betrayal for her memory.

Will came back into the room. The air wasn't so cool. He looked at the bed, replaying everything he could recall of his so very vivid dream. Did he just have his first intimate paranormal encounter? Or was it a surreal dream brought on by the slight infatuation he had for Saraphima, who bared a striking resemblance to his deceased fiance from so many years before? Anyone with a completely logical mind would lean towards the latter. Part of him wanted to think it was a paranormal experience, but until he was certain, he would write it off as a trick of the mind and an embarrassing wet dream.

Richard would be awake in an hour, and he needed to be at his peak for tonight, especially if he was going to take on the duo of termagants later that morning.

Dressed and ready to tackle the night and all the creatures that may dwell in its proverbial shadow-dwelling "things," Will closed his door behind him and made his way down the hall to Richard's room. He carried with him three laptops in their bags. Richard could work from his room tonight. It wasn't as big as Will's room, but it still had a big enough coffee table from which to operate.

The old grandfather clock chimed at 1:00 a.m. as Richard was sipping the coffee he had made in the kitchen and intently scanning his computer monitors. Will slipped from one monitor to the next and from one camera angle to another as he manoeuvred through the garden.

"Why the hell did we choose the garden again?" queried Will as he pressed his drowsy, scruffy face into one of the lenses.

Richard chuckled in amusement. "At least you're not in some grotesque basement or abandoned structure."

"Good call," the disembodied voice came over the headset. "Remember the hospital!?"

Richard took another sip. "I don't want to."

Now it was Will's turn to have a chuckle. "I'm not picking anything up out here. EVPs are running, and EMFs are normal. Shit! I'm even wearing a compass this time! This is rough!" he exclaimed as he traversed the garden, walking past the cameras and checking to see if they were still functioning.

On other investigations, the spirit would focus its attention or aggression on the cameras, knocking them over or draining their batteries within a fraction of their operating life.

"I'm tired," Will added.

Richard sipped his coffee again. "I can have a fresh brew for you when you get in." He wanted to ask Will if he was alright. His brother seemed distracted, which was a far cry from his normal agitations over pretty much anything, but they seemed amplified, especially with this place.

Richard's eyes and the camera lenses were in sync; through the computer monitors, he saw what they were watching, and both he and the panning cameras looked on intently. Through them, Richard studied everything as he moved from one lens to another with the press of a button on his laptops.

Kshhk.

"Try your EVP."

Kshhk.

He made this suggestion through Will's microphone as he studied the surroundings, every now and again catching a view of Will meandering through the gardens, seeming as though he was only half invested in the night. He watched as his brother stopped with an expression on his face that could only suggest why he didn't think of it. "Are you sure you're okay, brother? Usually, you're more intune with what is going on."

Will looked up at the camera blankly looking back at him with its singular, dull, lifeless eye. "I'm tired is all… It's nearly 1:40 in the fucking morning… I don't get why you're still up… How is the chest, by the way."

"It's good," Richard mused at his brother's frustrations. He always had. He watched Will remove the recorder from his vest pocket.

"I want to go to that little cemetery we saw earlier," he said. "It's just beyond the garden, on the east side of the drive…."

There was a moment of silence, and then, "Nope," came his brother's voice.

Will grunted in frustration but continued on his way. "Is there someone or something here tonight?" he said to his general surrounding, pausing. "Do you wish to communicate with us?" Silence.

"Why are you here?" he pressed on, rounding a corner.

Now Richard saw through the eye lenses that the entire mansion was in his view.

"Is there a reason why you're haunting the Law estate?" Nothing.

"Anything yet?" queried Will as he looked up at Richard's window.

"Nothing yet, Will. Your recorder and my computers are synced, so we should both be able to pick up the slightest EVP together. Do you have your earbuds in?"

"Yup, one," came a reply.

The camera fixed on Will spun around as he surveyed the grounds. "After all that has happened the past couple of days, how can things suddenly go quiet? Where the fuck are you?" he demanded sternly to the air.

"In your room," came a static, eerie voice crackling back.

Richard jumped, and apparently, Will did too as the camera image went shaky for a second before training to Richard's window. Then the lights went out.

"Holy shit! Did you hear that!?" Richard's voice said over the earpiece. "Get back here, now."

Will shuffled the recorder into his pocket and ran back to the mansion. He raced up the stairs and rounded the corner, surprised to see Richard standing outside his bedroom.

"Hear that?" Richard uttered silently as if trying not to disturb anyone or anything. "Something is going on in your room."

Will paused; there was a thumping noise emanating from behind his door. The closer he got, the louder it was until they were both standing before the door. A resounding *thump* was almost rhythmic and aggressive.

Will stared at Richard, who returned his bewildered gaze. Without a moment's hesitation, they threw open the heavy wooden door. Both the glider rocker and Will's bed were moving back and forth, striking the walls. The bed's wooden posts shuddered from the impact, and the sheets were strewn across the floor. A familiar odour permeated the room, and then everything stopped.

"Holy shit! It smells like sex in here," uttered Richard. "Did we just walk into ghost sex!?"

Will turned and looked at him, completely dumbfounded.

"We just disrupted two ghosts fucking in your bed!" mused Richard with a delighted expression on his face.

"Evidently, one was watching. That glider rocker was moving pretty vigorously," replied Will with equal enthusiasm.

"Are you getting laid?"

Will pretended he didn't hear his brother and proceeded to pour himself a scotch.

"There are documented cases of paranormal sensual encounters all over the globe," Richard continued.

"I'm not getting laid," responded Will as he sipped at his beverage, which calmed his nerves a bit. But as he said it, he could not help recall what had happened earlier and the state in which he awoke. This was new and somewhat embarrassing for him, and he was not about to let his brother place a camera in his room. He checked his EMF meter. The readings were a little high but nothing drastic; however, the temperature in the room was cool, which could be indicative of a paranormal entity manifesting itself or influencing objects.

They ventured back to Richard's room and played the recording back, and then again. After listening to the haunting words, they made a copy of it to play to Mrs. Law when next they met for breakfast. Richard copied the data onto a memory stick and placed it into Will's recording device. It played back wonderfully.

"Any sceptic would have a day with that and take great pleasure in vivisecting it, you know," said Richard as he handed his brother the EVR device.

"I know," was all Will could muster for a reply as he took the device.

Richard awoke after a few hours of sleep to Will's resounding voice echoing through the mansion's corridors. He lay unmoving, listening intently as if doubting that it could be his brother daring to raise his voice in such a way at a client's house, no matter how obtuse they were. It was when he heard the "F" word dropped in succession in a barrage of words that he threw himself from the warm sanctuary of his bed and into his breeches.

As he rushed down the hallway to the breakfast room, he could hear his brother expressing himself vibrantly. Pushing open the door, he was greeted by glares and stares of angry eyes. At the other end of the table stood Mrs. Law and Will.

Mrs. Law hardly broke her stately composure, with her nose turned upward at Will. At her back stood Lucy, quiet but equally furious, yet her expression harboured a modicum of amusement.

"Sit down, Mr. Stilton," demanded Mrs. Law of Richard. "From what I hear, you have had a trying night."

Richard nodded as he slowly manoeuvred himself into a chair and cautiously gazed at the trio until they were seemingly satisfied and resumed their morning meeting.

"I will not accept this photo, Mr. Stilton. It simply does not justify nor confirm anything I have contracted you for."

Will stood wide-eyed, flushed with anger as she continued.

"Your photos, therefore, are void of any consequence in this case."

Richard watched as the hints of a smile crept across Lucy's face, a sense of dark satisfaction or perhaps a small victory on her part for shunning the photo the night before.

Mrs. Law then trained her gaze on Richard, who looked up at her as a young child awaiting their scolding. "I understand you are the tech-savvy individual amongst the two of you?" Her tone expressed her utter distaste for technology.

If Richard did not know it before, he definitely knew it now.

"Look around you, Mr. Stilton. We are a people of a more dated time. Technology is not fully accepted around here, and I seldom understand it though I must, to a degree, for the sake of business. Though I typically leave that to the people who work for me, so I don't have to trouble myself with such tribulations. I am, however, aware that photographs can be manipulated on computers in this age of technology, and I, therefore, do not trust this photo."

Richard just stared back, slowly chewing his food, biting into his toast with his pinky finger out as if to appear proper.

"Are you listening to me, Mr. Stilton?"

Richard nodded.

"I do not understand your technology, nor do I care to. I utterly reject that grotesque voice on the toy your brother carries with him."

Will started to protest but was quickly shut down.

"You could have made that yourselves for all I know," she said as she turned her attention back to Will. "I am an individual of results, Mr. Stilton, and I expect them."

The two turned to exit the room.

Lucy stopped and briefly turned, looking back with a triumph in her eyes.

Richard smiled the biggest smile he could muster, his cheeks bulging with his breakfast and with that, she vacated the room.

Will sat down, frustrated and angry. He grasped for his already poured coffee, snatched a biscuit from a basket, and shoved it into his mouth. Not a word was spoken for a time as Will stared off into space. Richard, satisfied with his breakfast, watched Will stare blankly and was trying to figure out what he was staring at. Richard turned, trying to follow Will's line of vision. He turned back after scanning the room. What could he be so invested in? But there was only the room, complete with minimal decor. He glanced to the windows peering to the outside, but they were behind Will, and there was about as much going on out there as there was in the room. He soon returned his gaze to the breakfast room.

"What do we do now?" Richard boldly posed the query, breaking the mundane silence. No doubt he expected the worst from his brother, and Will was going to deliver it.

"We pack the van," he said resentfully, and that was it. He went for another biscuit.

Richard seemed to ponder for a moment as though reflecting on something distant yet not quite out of reach. "Didn't she already pay us a generous sum of money?"

Will was unmoving. "The cost of us to show up and our services rendered to date," he uttered begrudgingly and with a modicum of guilt as though trying to justify it to himself and his brother.

Richard smiled a large foolish grin. "You better say a proper fare-the-well to your gardener girl then."

Will shot Richard an undaunting glare. He was clearly amused at his own comment.

"What else do we have for audio? Anything?" Will changed the subject, and he was more than content to do so. As much as he welcomed and adored his brother's optimistic and peppy outlook on everything, there were times it was a little overbearing. Richard was a rock to him, and Will knew that he was self-destructive. If it wasn't for his brother, he could very well have hurt himself long ago or dug himself into a psychological hole that even he could not pull himself from. He was the best at what they did, and they both knew it, but Richard was his foundation and as much as he liked to think his brother knew that, Will wasn't entirely sure he did.

"Only what we have there," said Richard, pointing to the little voice recorder on the table. "Every time you've been out, if there were any form of audio, I would have picked it up.

Will looked hard at his brother. "Then we're done here. I'm sick of this shit. No amount of money is worth this amount of frustration and degradation."

Richard just nodded his head in agreement, no doubt knowing, by now, that there was no arguing with his brother when he got like this. "I'll start loading the van," was all he mustered as he sipped his morning coffee then rose from his chair.

Will watched his brother for a moment, then looked out the large window as if in contemplation. "Hold up."

Richard stopped and met Will's eyes, a tea biscuit half protruding from his mouth.

"I wouldn't mind checking out the family plot. I'd hate to depart without having the chance to sate my curiosity."

Richard nodded as he finished the biscuit. "It would be a shame," he stated in agreement.

"My give-a-fuck is completely depleted," continued Will.

"Never had I known that you did," said Richard in agreement.

Will shot him a look.

A half-cocky grin was laden across Richard's face.

"Fuck off," was all Will said with a half-smile.

"I will not!" Richard said, and with that, he left the room.

Will removed himself from the breakfast room and made his way to his bedroom. Although it was still early, he felt like he needed a drink. There is a distinct difference between needing and simply wanting, and after his morning meeting with Mrs. Law, he needed. Oh, how he needed!

After throwing open the door to his room, he charged over to the bottle and took a hardy swig of the peaty nectar and then one more just because, why not. He looked over the bottle in the direction of the family plot, then turned his attention to the gardens that garnished the landscape before his window. He then glanced back to the family plot. Will paused in thought. Why were the gardens maintained, and yet the family burial was so overgrown? This was a lack of attention, or so it seemed from where he stood.

Corking the bottle, he made his way to Richard's room, where his brother was slowly dismantling the computers he had set up on the floor. Richard looked up at Will as though searching for some regret to his decision to depart the Law estate. "We make hasty decisions when we're angry," he said, not taking his eyes off his brother.

Will looked down at him. His expression was unmoving and monotone, thinking. Will walked around his brother and trained his eyes out the window again, now completely transfixed by the idea of exploring the family cemetery.

"What's changing your mind?" uttered Richard. "The gardener, the cemetery, or the idea of leaving a job unfinished and completely tarnishing your record?"

Will heard his brother but chose not to respond right away. Instead, he just turned his attention back to the gardens that were in the front yard of the estate.

"Mayhaps a little of everything," was his response. He turned to Richard, who was now sitting upright, the computer cords all bound neatly in front of him, ready to be put away in their respective cases.

"It's not easy," Richard said, "to be challenged so fervently and rejected so passionately in what it is that you do so well. Our business is not an easy one." He paused for a moment. "Then to find out that the client is a giant bitch who has no intention of regarding our past for what it is and chooses not to see us nor the company for what it is. She utterly expects us to go against everything we have worked so hard to explore and accomplish purely for the benefit of her estate and to prove her workers false in all of their accusations."

He then looked at Will hard. If Richard, this jovial giant of a man, had a serious voice, this was it.

Richard continued, "Then meeting a girl that you hadn't ever planned on meeting and completely finding yourself drawn to her. You are enchanted by everything that she is, and you only see her on her terms. Someone from our walk of life might almost consider her…"

Will had now turned and was looking at his brother hard, with no malice, just intently because as much as he would love to disagree with Richard, a lot of times, he made good sense of things that would leave Will guessing or undecided.

"A ghost, one might speculate." Richard finished with the hint of a smile on the corners of his lips.

Will didn't even try to argue. "A ghost in the sense of not always being around, and I seem to find myself in the right place at the right time? Or a ghost as in the ethereal sense, and in which case, who you gonna call? Because it sure as hell isn't us right now."

Richard, smiling, started individually plugging the computers back in and booting them up one by one. "So we are going to hit the family cemetery tonight then?" he posed as he booted up the last of his laptops.

Will smiled wryly. "Yes, we're going to the family plot tonight. But I swear I'm at my wits end with that shit of a lady."

"Who, may I inquire, is a, how you so eloquently put it, 'shit of a lady'?" Came a voice from the door of their room.

Richard spun about, and Will turned his eyes upward to see Lucy standing in their doorway, a hard look glaring back at them.

"If I may ask?"

Will was quick to pounce. "Well, I'm sure as fuck not talking about you. You'd have to be a lady!" A cocky grin crept across his face as he said it, a sense of self-satisfaction welling up within him.

She glared at Will with fierce resentment. "Thin walls, Mr. Stilton." She then looked down at Richard. "Do keep your brother under control. His mouth must continually get him in trouble."

Richard simply smiled and winked in reply.

Lucy's cheeks flushed slightly, and Will couldn't tell if it was through bashfulness or anger.

"If you are seeking entry into the family cemetery, Mr. Stilton, then you should know that it is gated. There is a key that hung in Mrs. Law's late husband's study. It is a large skeleton key. Since Mr. Law's passing, his study has been moved to another room on the west end of the building. If it isn't there, it might have been placed in the old carriage house. No one ventures in the cemetery anymore, not since Mr. Law's demise."

Both Will and Richard were looking at her, completely astounded by her sudden change in attitude toward them. She'd gone from this angry, resentful right hand of the lady of the estate to this resentful and seemingly helpful right hand.

"Most of the doors in this place are locked," uttered Will, a harshness in his tone.

"Mrs. Law already stated it, and I'm sure I've tried every doorknob," Lucy regarded him tartly. "Then I will unlock it." She paused for a moment. "I'd move swiftly. Doors in this place have a tendency to lock and unlock themselves at times."

"So you admit something is going on in this place?" blurted Richard accusatorily.

"I admit nothing, Mr. Stilton," she snapped abrasively, shooting them a look of animosity.

"What are you playing at, lady," uttered Will.

She looked at him as if not understanding the question.

"You have been nothing but hate and a giant pain in the ass since we arrived under the employ of *your* employer, and now you want to help us out?"

"What is with the sudden change of heart?" chimed Richard. "Is what my brother is trying to convey."

Her eyes darted between the both of them. "The sooner you are gone, the sooner things go back to normal, so when you are done poking around, then you can jump into your van and travel home and continue chasing your ghosts elsewhere."

"And what is your idea of normalcy?" continued Will. "With all the shit we've seen here, there is no way you haven't seen anything. There is something beyond the scope of two paranormal investigators afoot at the Law estate."

Lucy paused in thought, or she was merely digesting what her guest had posed to her. Then regaining her composure, she said, "Normalcy, Mr. Stilton, is not having you and your brother here."

Will caught his brother's glance as she continued.

"You are here for the workers, Mr. Stilton, to sate their fancies, to keep them in Mrs. Law's employ. Nothing more."

Will simply nodded and thanked Lucy for her contribution, then watched her take her leave.

"What do you think?" whispered Richard, his eyes still trained on his brother.

Will looked down at him in silence for a moment. "Get this working," he directed at the computers meticulously scattered on the floor. "I really want to know what is in that family cemetery."

"We can get the key from the room where the late Mr. Law's study had been relocated." Replied Richard with a faint smile. "We might find something useful, perhaps from when he was alive?"

Will nodded in agreement as he slipped the cork back into the bottle. "We can head to the study, and if we don't find the key, then we make our way to the carriage house."

Richard nodded in concurrence.

CHAPTER NINE

REVELATION

Will led the way as he and Richard walked about the west end of the mansion, looking for the room Mr. Law's study had been moved to. Testing every door they came to, they found many were still locked, but those that were unlocked yielded nothing more than well-maintained bedrooms as though they were waiting for occupants to arrive shortly. Will checked over the furniture and other flat surfaces, noting that it was all regularly dusted and cleaned. Some rooms seemed to carry the odour of ammonia or some other cleaning products as though, despite the regular maintenance, they had very recently been tended to.

Despite Will's agitated protests, Richard went so far as to look for hidden rooms or passages by pulling on sconces or books, but he stood firm in his belief that large mansions such as the Law estate always had secrets in their secrets. Exiting a room, Will heard a *click*. He paused in the hall. "Did you hear that?" he said, looking up to Richard, who clearly had as he stared down the corridor.

Click.

The brothers glanced at one another briefly, then hurried down the hall, grasping at the doorknobs. Will reached for one door.

Click.

It locked before he could grab it. "Bugger me!" he uttered as he grasped another one.

Click.

It locked in his hand. "Fuck!" he bellowed in frustration.

Soon the corridor was filled with the resounding *clicks* of the multitude of doors locking and unlocking simultaneously, and then everything went silent.

Despite his agitation, Will was content to watch his brother work out his own frustrations on the uncooperative doorknobs. One gave in under his brutish strength with a *snap* as he grabbed the doorknob with two hands and twisted it aggressively. With a jerk, both the knob and the spindle with it came out in his hand, followed by a *thud,* as the knob and shank on the other side fell to the floor. Peering in the room, he saw that it was filled with porcelain dolls, from floor to ceiling. Some looked too new to have been sitting for a long period of time. All of their expressions, with their rosy cheeks, assorted smiles, realistic skin tones, and painted-on eyes, were glaring at the door as though eerily waiting for their master to walk in. It was a room filled with tiny children frozen in time. Some were facing a chair in the centre of the room, and beside it was a small table with a brush and a plastic tea set on it.

"I think we found Mrs. Law's children," uttered Will as they peered in, not wanting to completely cross the threshold.

"She could just be a collector," stated Richard, who looked down to meet Will's gaze as he was looking up. They decided not to go into it any further and wrote this room off as a bust. Richard pulled the door shut as best he could and gingerly slid the doorknob and spindle back in its place. The door stood slightly ajar, but the brothers moved on as if they hadn't noticed it.

Richard managed to wrestle another doorknob off. The second room looked as though it had never seen use. It was old and damp with the scent of mildew in the air. Dank and desolate, the room must not have been entered for quite some time. Cobwebs occupied the corners of the ceiling and hung from the legs of the table in the middle of the room. A bassinet lay under the window, below drawn, threadbare curtains. The bassinet looked frail from years of sun exposure and was shrouded in cobwebs that stretched to the curtains. Against a wall was a bed with four bedposts, musty with age. Cobwebs hung from the bedposts in wisps like forgotten ghosts that could never rest. Thick layers of dust occupied the flat surfaces and clung to the cobwebs, making them drape like tattered curtains. There was such a heavy, looming sadness about the room that they both nearly regretted opening the door. Richard neatly pulled the door shut as he did with the previous door, leaving this room's secrets to itself.

"The hell with this," said Will, completely vexed. "We'll be at this forever." He sighed. "Let's make our way to the carriage house." He looked at Richard as if he were waiting for his brother's approval. Richard nodded in agreement, also feeling defeated.

"We're definitely not wanted here," he said, pointing at one of the broken doorknobs victoriously.

The brothers pushed their way through the large wooden doors and made their way down the steps. The shuffling of feet on concrete turned to the crunching of gravel underfoot. Will looked over to the fountain. Part of him was hoping to see Saraphima there neatly tending to her lilies, but a wave of disappointment rushed over him when she was not. Suddenly, Will's eyes widened with an epiphany.

"Hold up," said Will as he put one hand on Richard's shoulder, who turned to face him.

"Do you think this place has a basement?"

Richard regarded his brother for a second. "It's a possibility!" he replied with a modicum of intrigue in his voice. "Most of the time, these older structures just have a dug-out basement or cold cellar, not a real basement per se."

Will nodded. "But what if it did have at least a partial basement with access via outdoor bulkhead doors?" Will stood with a cocky grin as if he were happy with his idea.

Richard regarded him with a queer expression. "Sounds intriguingly creepy."

"I'm not trying to be creepy; I'm trying to do my job or whatever the fuck I'm supposed to be here for," retorted Will, slightly annoyed at the way his brother was regarding him.

Richard paused, as if thinking, then continued, "What if I went to the carriage house and you quickly looked for the bulkhead doors that could potentially be a basement." He mockingly threw up his fingers in quotation marks.

Will's expression hardened, an air of agitation on his brow. "What is that supposed to mean?"

"If there is indeed a key in the carriage house, then we can grab that because we sure as hell aren't finding it in the west end." Richard brandished a smile and nodded as his brother spoke.

"And if there *are* bulkhead doors and there *is* at least something of a basement, then maybe the contents of the late Mr. Law's study are in there?" Will paused. "Or maybe there is something even bigger! I don't entirely trust Lucy. She's all kinds of fuckary."

"Uh-huh," said Richard suspiciously. "Let me know if you run into your gardener lady. I'd like to meet her!" He cheerily watched Will's face flush a light red. "Busted!" Richard said with a victorious guffaw as Will hung his head, slightly dismayed he'd been figured out.

Will navigated the mansion's overgrown hedges from the gardens. They obscured the walls and the foundation. He spent time studying what features he could make out. Many of the windows that faced the noon sun reflected the outside, making the estate appear dark and forlorn inside.

As he walked, he looked up at the second-story windows, looming and dark, hoping to whatever god there is that there would be bulkhead doors jutting from the foundation of this forsaken place so that he could at least throw it back at Richard.

"Shit!" he exclaimed to himself as he stood looking at the myriad of bushes and overgrown shrubs concealing the mansion's foundation. Will had not made his way around the entire ground floor of the estate yet, but it was proving tougher than he thought. He looked to the west where the orchard was. He could hear the bustling of chatty workers earning their wages by plucking from the trees. Tractors puttered about, their wagons overloaded with bushels and full to the brim with apples. Everyone was hustling before the Autumn season came to a close and before the birds and pathogens took their share.

Making his way around the mansion, he was now looking to the east. He could see a vineyard as far as his eyes would allow. Figures meticulously moved throughout the rows of vines, methodically plucking the grapes and hoarding them in their baskets. Tractors puttered there, too, towing their burdened wagons. He watched them for a minute, thankful he was not one of them and turned back to his task in finding bulkhead doors, but really, he was keeping a watchful eye for Saraphima. It was foolish to try to pull the proverbial wool over Richard's eyes. He was far too smart, even if he did have every intention of finding a basement entrance.

It was a haven for the mosses and lichens where the stone was constantly shunned from the sunlight. Cool and damp, it grew from the trees and hung off the stone walls in large columns, thriving in the bitter shade.

Will, meandering about the mansion, hadn't entirely given up on the idea of a basement, but he was looking about as if surveying the area. His mind wandered continually to the other night. He could still hear her voice in his head, softly telling him to awaken. He could still feel her touch and her deep breaths and sighs on his skin. But he could not recall any warmth to her at all. The sensuality was so real, and the moment was stunningly hot, but he could not recall any warmth. Had he encountered his first sexual paranormal experience? Had it just been a wet dream that was so vivid it excited his senses in his sleep? There were investigators that would throw themselves at the chance to experience a sensual ghostly phenomenon, but he still was uncertain.

He was nearing the end of the building when came a voice, a welcoming, warm voice that he recognized immediately. Will turned to see Saraphima.

She was still dressed in her blue overalls with dirty knees, lightly dirty shoes, and her small hands bore gardening gloves. Her hair was slightly pulled back, but curly locks hung freely here and there. Her eyes were wide with intrigue as she smiled her pretty smile.

"Are you lost, Mr. Stilton?" she queried as she chuckled to herself.

Will's cheeks were suddenly flushed with red. He could try to expound it to getting caught prowling around the building, but he knew it was Saraphima, and he was damn sure she knew it too.

"We were trying to find the late Mr. Law's study." He hoped he didn't appear too smitten. "Apparently, the study was moved after Mr. Law's demise. According to Lucy, Mr. Law kept a key to the cemetery there. She also stated that if it wasn't in the study, it should be in the carriage house."

She looked at Will quizzically as he spoke.

"I had the notion that there might be an old basement where the contents of the study may have been moved to, and given the age of the estate, this place may have basement access via exterior bulkhead doors." He paused to look at the building then gazed back to Saraphima. "We're hoping that maybe there might be something useful in it. My brother is on his way to the carriage house for the cemetery key."

Saraphima looked intrigued. "Oh! So you are a sleuth as well as a paranormal expert!" she mused.

Will smiled at her playful nature, and he didn't want to. He grew serious. "Do you know anything?" he queried.

Saraphima's smile faded to almost a cocky smirk as though she did know something but would only divulge on her terms. "It is no secret that Mr. and Mrs. Law both had a mind for business. While Mrs. Law handled everything to do with the estate, Mr. Law looked after the workers. Their relationship seemed almost nonexistent at times."

Will was invested in what she had to say, but he almost didn't feel surprised about the state of Mrs. Law's relation with her late husband. Who could love that after all? A small smile crept on his lips.

"Do you find that amusing, Mr. Stilton?" asked Saraphima, observing his foolish smile.

"I do not," he said, checking himself, so he wasn't standing there grinning like an idiot.

She continued, "After the death of Mr. Law, Mrs. Law turned his study into a bedroom. I mean, he already had a bed in there for when he worked late hours. It was the one place he could be where his wife cared not to go. Most of his things were taken to Mrs. Law's personal library, but many of the items from the study were incinerated where they burn the trimmings from the trees or clippings from the vines." She pointed to the northeast, off to the corner of the estate. "There is no basement here, Mr. Stilton."

Will's eyes grew wide, and his jaw was slightly slack. "Do you happen to know where this bedroom is?"

An ill-feeling rushed over Will, and he almost felt as though he was going to be sick, but he stifled the reflex. "Holy shit!" was all he could say.

"Indeed, Mr. Stilton." She leaned a little closer to Will. "As kind a soul as Mr. Law was, and he was kind to all of the working staff and workers out in the fields, he did relish having company in his study from time to time." She stepped back as Will regarded her with a grand sense of intrigue. "It must be hard to be married and yet so alone," she said.

"I can only imagine." Will was taken aback at the way Saraphima regarded him. For a moment, his thoughts drifted to Brynn. A cryptozoologist, Brynn's passion for her career led Will to spend many nights alone while she was working on something fantastical at the museum. He knew he was never truly alone, but after her passing, part of him wanted to pretend she was at work and would come home soon. He was unwilling to accept the cruel reality.

He gazed on Saraphima in wonderment. Where and how did she become privy to such information undoubtedly censored from the general labourer. "Is there anything else you want to tell me?" he said with an inquisitive tone designed to urge the gardener to give up more secrets.

Saraphima studied him for a moment and, with a smile, said, "Nope! I've said what I wanted to. Now, if you will excuse me, Mr. Stilton."

Will nodded. "Of course." He might have watched her disappear behind the bushes, but Will turned to head back to Richard.

"Mr. Stilton!" Will turned to see Saraphima in the distance. "It was nice, though, wasn't it?"

Will looked on, raising an eyebrow without a word.

"The other night, William. Wasn't it nice?"

Will dazed out for a brief moment but quickly came to. "Oh yes! It was really nice!"

Saraphima smiled and began to turn away.

"Which part, my dear?" Will shouted after her.

She turned to face him again.

"Which part of the night was nice?" Will felt his brow wrinkling. The previous night was wrought with so much activity, both physical and metaphysical, that he just had to ask no matter how unorthodox the query seemed.

Saraphima simply smiled. "Why, Mr. Stilton, I would think all of it." She turned and walked off.

Kshhk
"Richard, are you there?"
Kshhk

Kshhk
"I'm here," came Richard's familiar voice. "Will, I'm in the carriage house. You have to come here. There is something you have to see."
Kshhk

Will started back the way he came.

Kshhk
*"Where is it?"
Kshhk

Kshhk
"Not far, near the end of the drive, but go east of the building."
Kshhk

Will hurriedly made his way to the end of the drive then followed Richard's directions until he came to the old carriage house. It was in need of repair but not so far gone that one would consider it condemned. The roof alone looked only to be a few years old despite the weather damage to the stonework, and the door appeared sturdy enough.

It creaked as Richard opened it up. Horror and excitement was all over his face. "You have to see this."

Then he disappeared back inside, in the darkness beyond the walls, and Will was quick to follow.

The inside was musty. It smelt of cut grass, rusted metal, and the decay of old wooden beams. Will followed his brother past an old tractor covered in grass clippings and, to his bemusement, a carriage! It appeared to be Victorian by the bustling wooden floral carvings that adorned the four corners of the carriage, reaching down to the coachman's seat and down its skeleton boot, ending at the coachman's step. Layers of dust obscured what must have once been a polished obsidian finish. The springs and futchells looked as though they would be seized from years of rust, and he could see the deep pits in the roller bolt and splinter bar. This had most definitely been a gem back in its day, but now it was just another hidden secret suffering the decay of time. Just beyond the carriage was an old Delta, beige or cream white. It was hard to tell with the layers of dust and age that had accumulated on it.

"Look at this," Richard said, motioning to the front of the car.

Will leaned over the hood of the Delta; the front end was damaged, the driver's side headlight was smashed, and the bumper was pushed in. The hood had a slight dent in it, and the driver's mirror was missing.

Richard raised his camera to his face and began snapping photos of the vehicle while wiping the windows to see inside. He tested the doors, but they were all locked.

"Is this what you wanted to show me? This is what got you excited? An old Delta?"

Richard regarded his brother for a moment, and his face was more serious than Will had ever seen before. He put his hand to his chest. "I'm telling you, Will, that woman the other night, she was hit by a car, no doubt about it. And now look what we find—an old car with a smashed front end."

Will just stood there for a moment, digesting what Richard was saying.

"She was wearing a nightgown, but on this desolate stretch of road between here and town, why would she be out running through the forest!?" He paused. "Dammit, Will! You weren't there. You didn't see what I saw. My damn chest says it all!"

Now Will's expression mirrored Richard's. He was absolutely right.

"There is more here than just a haunting," continued Richard, "and I'm starting to think we have found ourselves in some kind of trouble."

As his brother spoke, Will was taking note that the temperature in the carriage house was dropping.

Richard hushed as their breath was becoming noticeably visible. Their exhales were vaporous plumes that licked their cheeks then dissipated.

Before either could say anything, the car shuddered, the engine sputtered, and the headlight flickered on then off again, flashing the investigators. Will and Richard jumped back as the Delta convulsed, trying to lurch forward, its engine sputtering and its lights flickering. Plumes of sooty exhaust billowed from the tailpipe as the car wrenched and jerked. Moving parts squeaked and moaned. Then it fell silent. The brothers were gobsmacked. They stood for a moment in the silence before Richard playfully tapped Will on the back of the head.

"Explain that away, detective," he said tauntingly, but Will was not phased by the taunt or that he could taste the exhaust. Instead, he merely looked up at Richard.

"Can you feel that?" Will uttered, and Richard quickly ceased his mockery.

They felt the air grow colder.

Their breath was becoming more visible with each exhale, mixing with the sooty vapours that lingered. With each breath, the air grew colder, and soon he and Richard were exhaling long silky clouds of their own that twisted and swirled in the now-bitter air. Will fumbled through his pockets: no EMF meter, but he did have a compass and an infrared thermometer. Holding out the compass, Will noted the needle was spinning steadily around. As he neared the car, he carefully placed the compass on the hood, and he and Richard watched as the compass spun almost uncontrollably.

Will pointed the infrared thermometer at the car and shot a laser onto it for a reading. "Holy shit," he muttered.

The car was registering as minus eight degrees Celsius. Will's heart thudded, and a quick glance at Richard revealed his horrific expression as blood began to trickle from the car's grill and smashed headlight, running down the bumper and pooling on the floor at their feet. Richard took another picture and joined Will in a crouched position, both kneeling before the collecting blood on the cold concrete floor. It was as viscous as a syrup, dripping and pouring in small intervals, steadily increasing the puddle.

Will placed a finger in the thick, nearly coagulated blood. It was immensely cold to the touch, and he withdrew quickly.

"Have we ever seen anything like this?" he asked, but Richard shook his head, still obviously stricken with amazement and horror.

The headlights of the car suddenly turned on. Will stumbled back and tried to regain his footing, but Richard fell over him. They clamoured to their feet while shielding their eyes in an attempt to shut out the light. A loud scream was followed by a crash, and the sounds of twisting metal mixed with the stretching of sinew and crunching of bones resonated through the carriage house, filling the cold air and echoing in Will's ears. Then the lights went out.

Standing in the pitch dark, with vision blurred and obstructed, Will struggled to look around him and noticed Richard standing nearly frozen. His breathing became heavier as he placed a hand on Will's shoulder. He rubbed his eyes with his other hand. Finally, a sound came, like a churning, gargling hiss, as though someone was choking and trying to speak.

"Do you hear that?" Richard asked Will in a low, near whisper.

Will nodded in reply. "Yeah, I do, but I can't see shit."

Richard's grip tightened as though if he held his brother tightly enough somehow, they would both be safe. "That's it! That's the sound, Will. The woman."

Will paused for a moment, and their vision had returned.

The brothers found themselves glaring at the car, still mangled but atop its hood and sprawled out broken and bleeding, was the entity. She glared back in unmatched fury and terror. Blood spewed and trickled from her gaping mouth as she struggled to speak. Her body, broken and bent, covered the spiderweb of cracks in the windshield. She was scratching at the paint where nail marks already were, stricken, like a beast trying to claw free from the clutches of a trap. There was a horror in her panic, her fury, as she slowly began to dissipate, and as quickly as she appeared, she faded. But the blood, residual as ectoplasm, remained. The hood was left glossy in a thick slimy substance that Will and his brother had seen before, but only once, and it was an extreme case.

"Bloody hell!" Will exclaimed aloud, not knowing what to do next.

Richard reacted first, as though not phased by the apparition or motivated purely out of fear, and began rummaging through the carriage house. The clanging of tools and implements pulled Will from his awe-struck state. He grasped his compass from off the car and helped his brother rummage.

Richard withdrew from a cabinet a rusty iron ring adorned with a plethora of keys. Older and newer keys hung from the ring as Richard held it out for his brother to see. "Now, let's get the hell out of here," he nearly demanded as he ushered Will from the building and into the daylight.

As the two drank in the air that was not polluted with the aromas of the carriage house or the exhaust from the car,

Will regaled his brother with the story of his encounter with Saraphima and what she had told him.

"Holy shit!" Richard blurted.

"My words exactly," said Will as the duo made their way to the old cemetery on the east side of the grounds, roughly seventy yards from the entrance to the estate. The gates were locked, just as Lucy had foretold, and the surrounding fence was overrun with vines and grasses. Tree branches pushed through the old iron bars or draped over the fence as if in an attempt to conceal it from prying eyes. Beyond the gate, it looked as though the cemetery had been managed and manicured but not recently.

Richard tested key after key until there came the successful *click* as the lock sprang open. The gates creaked as they swung open, and vines and grasses stretched and strained as they were pulled inward, refusing to relinquish their grip. Will was awestruck as they meandered into the cemetery. Old tombstones hardly visible from behind the fence now came into view, peeking over tall grasses that threatened to consume them. Tall evergreen trees and the odd oak or beech cast a permanent shadow over the burial site, their branches and leaves caressing and littering the three mausoleums that stood stoic against the ravages of time.

As Richard made his way to the headstones, Will manoeuvred to the mausoleums. Placing his fingertips on the old pitted stonework, he looked for any kind of date, something to tell him when it was erected or even a ledger of who may be entombed within, but he found nothing on either. Stepping up to the entrance, he examined the small metal doors, befitting a small entryway, just large enough to allow only one person entry or exit at a time. Will would only have to duck slightly to get in, but Richard would have a much harder time with the height of the archway. The doors were arched to match the shape of the entryway and where they met in the middle, adorned with a large, heavy built-in lock. He rocked each door slightly, and each swayed slightly under the force. The door itself was thin, but the lock was almost too heavy for such a door. It was pitted and rusted, and there were no marks in the large keyhole to suggest it had been actively opened or closed recently. Decorative brass garnished the door, stained green from time and slight decay.

As Will moved from one mausoleum to the next, he noticed all three had similar features: small windows that lined the sides to let in a modicum of light and thin wire bars embedded in the glass, no doubt for keeping grave robbers and other seekers from gaining entry. The Law name featured on a massive keystone over the entrance, and each roof appeared to be in a state of disrepair. If they were built years apart, he could not tell, for they all exhibited the same structural decay. With not a date on one nor an accounting of who may be entombed inside, truly they were mysteries.

"Hey! Will!" called Richard.

Will's attention turned in his brother's direction to see him standing amidst the tall grasses and headstones. Abandoning his curiosity with the burial structures, Will made his way to his brother, who was now rummaging through the grasses, pulling up broken pieces of a headstone, scattered and partly sunken in the earth obscured by the grass.

"Who could do this and why?" posed Richard, holding up a broken piece of headstone, not waiting for an answer.

Will watched his brother pull another large piece of headstone from an entanglement of grasses, prying it from the earth that was slowly reclaiming it. At Will's feet was the base of the gravestone. Its edges were still rough from where it had been torn asunder but littered with lichen that fed on the calcium from the stone.

"There is another broken headstone behind that old evergreen." Richard pointed at the old tree trunk just out of Will's reach as he stood over the desecrated gravestone.

"I haven't found any others, just these two," said Richard, labouring over the stone pieces. "But what would drive someone to destroy two gravestones? Especially in a family plot?"

Will didn't say anything. He made his way over to the other ravaged gravestone and found fragments littered about. He bent down and rummaged through the debris, rolling over the larger pieces still glossy and flat from where they were manicured, despite the rough edges. One piece, a large concave impact indentation, scored the stone's surface. The glossy, nearly glassy finish was shattered from the impact. Another piece exhibited a similar impact, distorting a letter. Will leaned over it, picking and cleaning, his sense of intrigue now beyond piqued. He discovered an "RA." He pulled over another one. "S."

Will's heart suddenly sank as a chill rushed through him. He stumbled back and fell against the tree, and nausea came over him as he glared at the two letters sprawled in the grass. He wanted to keep going, but he was scared of what he might find.

"Bloody hell!" came Richard's voice behind him.

After a minute, Will clamoured to his feet and looked over to see Richard standing over the gravestone, awaiting his attention.

Looking at Will, Richard pointed downward. "Take a look at this." Richard then abandoned the gravestones and was now intently testing the keys in the locks of the mausoleums.

Curious, Will made his way to the broken headstone that Richard had assembled in some crude fashion, just enough to make it legible.

Edgar Law.

Half of the "W" was missing, but it was safe to assume. The rest of the headstone must have taken the brunt of the impact as it was smashed into tiny fragments scattered through the grasses, and who knew how far they spread out. No one simply smashes a headstone and keeps it contained in a neat little pile.

Will shook his head, partly in disgust and partly in annoyance at whoever could be capable of committing such a violation against something so sacred. Unless… it wasn't sacred.

"Bugger!"

Will turned to see Richard had exhausted all of the keys on the third mausoleum without success. The other two, their doors were swung open and free to explore. To many, the idea of an open mausoleum may be morbid, but Will and Richard found it was quite inviting.

With his curiosity revived, he meandered over to the first mausoleum. Within its walls lay three concrete caskets, dry and dusty.

Litter and debris that managed to blow under the door had laid undisturbed until they had stirred it up. Were they violating the sanctity of the crypt? Will didn't care. With all of the events that had taken place and Mrs. Law's refusal to accept the evidence, his "give a shit" had plummeted. If Mrs. Law were anyone but herself, they would have a persistent presence at the estate. It's a hot spot of paranormal activity. Will knew it. He could feel it, and with everything that had transpired so far, how could he even begin to deny it! It was blatantly in their faces, so how could it be so unnoticed by Ol' Lady Law… he was growing fond of that phrase…

But despite everything, he wouldn't say it just yet. Unbeknownst to Richard, he was still struggling with the amoral decision to just tell Lady Law what she wanted to hear, collect their dues, and be done with it. But he would be betraying his own morals and, worst of all, Richard's and the Stilton Paranormal Research Institute.

The second mausoleum was very much the same as the first. Everything was undisturbed before they entered the concrete chamber that housed two concrete caskets and a small number of urns laden in the walls.

"We have never been in the business of desecrating the dead," he exclaimed as he placed the vessel back in its resting spot. His tone was strict and absolute.

Will wanted to argue, and he knew that his brother was equally as curious. "Any luck with the third mausoleum?" he posed instead as he made his way to the door.

"Nothing. Not a single key worked." Richard looked defeated as he held up the rings of the variety of old and modern keys.

Will made his way to the second mausoleum with his brother in tow, and together, a second attempt was made to no avail. Will pointed out the broken window, and Richard raised his eyebrow and got that gleam in his eye, but in the end, the mausoleum stood defiant, and its secrets remained hidden. Now, Will was as equally defeated as his brother. They stood gazing at the long grasses swaying in the light breeze, revealing glimpses of tombstones hidden in the sea of browns and greens with the light colours of those going to seed. The branches of trees danced up and down in large circles in sync with the swaying grasses. Their branches caressed some of the headstones, mostly those that were covered in mosses and lichens. Together, they were an undulating beast, and in its maw were the stone teeth that bore the names of those deceased.

"Has Mrs. Law ever mentioned her late husband's name?" posed Will, not removing his eyes from the spot where the two tombstones were smashed.

Richard pondered the query for a moment. "I do not believe she has," he uttered in response, eyes fixed on the dancing field. Shadows of the trees, grasses, and headstones stretched in the fading sunlight, creeping across the pathway and pointing toward the gate as though it were an ethereal message to the brothers to take their leave.

"Do you think he was Edgar Law?" asked Richard as they started to make their way to the cemetery gate.

"Maybe," said Will. "But why smash the headstone?" he added. Will was still annoyed about the urn and the smashed marker bearing the letters "RA and "S," yet, despite his annoyance, he was eager to upload the camera SD card into one of Richard's computers, and he knew that Richard couldn't wait to see what he captured too. Will didn't want to admit nor show that he was still shaken from their time inside the carriage house, excited yet shaken nonetheless.

Richard pushed his way into the bedroom first, and he felt Will knock him from behind, reminiscent of two young men fighting for last call at the local pub. Richard nearly threw himself to his equipment on the floor while Will fiercely strode to the bottle of scotch which was the only thing that stood out in his room at that moment. The computers roared to life one by one as Richard hastily pushed the SD card in its appropriate slot and let the machines do their magic. With a multitude of *clicks* and *taps*, he pulled up the photos of the carriage house.

Will flopped beside him, and Richard scrolled through picture after picture. He felt like they were two boys looking at forbidden adult magazines for the first time. The carriage house was even more foreboding in the pictures, and the damage on the Delta was vivid, appearing as though it had just happened.

Then there she was. They almost recoiled when the first picture came to view. Her wretched face was crying out, her twisted and mangled body wrapped around the car. Her eyes were haunting and horrific as she glared at them and nothing at the same time. The blood that flowed from her gaped mouth ran onto the hood of the vehicle with the rest of the bloody ectoplasm that pooled on the bumper and the floor. And then she was gone, and there was only a picture of a damaged car with a dark glossy plasma puddled on the hood.

Richard leaned back, propping himself against the foot of the bed, and watched Will hoist the bottle high towards the door as though Lucy or Mrs. Law were standing in the threshold.

"Here's a heaping helping of go fuck yourselves!" he announced and proceeded to imbibe, then handed the bottle to Richard, who hoisted it in the same fashion.

"To Lucy. May her love for me never come true!" He and Will laughed, relishing in their private victory, still revelling in their encounter.

"We can't show this to Mrs. Law. She wouldn't believe us anyway. We would be accused of being frauds again," said Richard as he handed the bottle back to Will.

"Indeed," was his only response as he stood in thought for a moment with a few more sips to follow. "What do we know about Ol' Lady Law's character?" said Will, finally breaking the silence. "She's a wealthy, successful but shifty, cold, demeaning, arrogant tosser of 'old money wealth' that is used to getting her way presumably at any price." He paused.

Richard was regarding him sceptically. "What's on the line for us in this investigation?"

Will continued, "The thing is, she could attack directly if we simply say outright, 'Yup! This place has no paranormal activity at all!' telling her what she apparently wants to hear rather than throwing all of this evidence her way quite to the contrary."

Richard found himself glaring at his brother in astonishment. How had neither one of them thought of it before? "Our reputation, our credibility as paranormal investigators," he said as he snatched the bottle from his brother's grasp. "Not only would we be under intense scrutiny from the paranormal community for not standing behind our beliefs, but we may also be branded as sellouts."

"Exactly," said Will.

They both knew the severity of such an accusation could be devastating. Richard took a swig. "The scientific communities that have no regard for the supernatural, ethereal, or fantastical would pick us apart no matter how much evidence we've accumulated. Our report with paranormal investigative firms or societies would stand to be tarnished... possibly."

"Absolutely," agreed Will. "This is all hypothetical, based on the idea that Ol' lady Law does, in fact, try to muddy our reputation."

"So we do what we do best until the job is done," said Richard almost defiantly.

Will smiled. "Absolutely. We get as much evidence as we can muster, and we present as usual until the job is done." He thought for a moment. "It's a damn creepy place, this estate. It's one of the most active places we've been to."

Richard nodded. "Given what we've seen, there is something bigger than just a haunt; there is a history."

Will turned and looked out the window at the night sky, at the forest, at the fountain, and toward the carriage house. "I sense something foul in the air, brother." He turned his gaze on Richard. "And I'm not entirely sure if it's the spirits or this place itself... or Mrs. Law."

The spirits, Will thought to himself. He already vocalized it and couldn't take it back, not now. He had already come to terms with the realization that this place was haunted some time ago. *Richard, saturated in the bedroom and the chairs in the ballroom being tossed about. The blood on the door and the photograph of the woman, face down in the fountain and now this old car, erupting to life with the broken phantasmal body of a tortured soul sprawled on its spiderweb cracked windshield and scratched hood.* The thoughts chased each other through his mind as he looked up at his brother. He knew Richard heard him acknowledge the spirits, but he was doing an equally good job at pretending he hadn't noticed...

"About time you came around," he stated with his big smile and happy eyes.

And there it is. The phrase shot through Will's mind as though it were eagerly waiting its turn.

"Maybe you can get the number of that gardener lady before we finish up here," said Richard playfully. "I think she's the best thing about this place... of course, I haven't seen her, and I can tell you're smitten."

Will smiled. "Maybe," was all he said, but in the back of his mind, he felt that she was still a part of this place, that if they offered to take her away from the estate and the dreary town of Brackenstone, she'd probably turn them down. He looked out the window in the direction of her cabin, then back to Richard. "Wouldn't that be nice," said Will before changing the subject and soon they were reminiscing on cases that brought them chills and left memorable sensations until it was time to retire for the night.

CHAPTER TEN

FIND ME

Soft fingers gently ran down the length of his arm and up from his naval. Will shuddered in his slumber as they traversed his ribs up to his chest. The touch was eerily cool as they moved in sensual intensity. Nipples, like two cold drops of water, kissed his back, then the fullness of breasts pressed into him. An arm bound about his torso, tight, comforting, and somewhat familiar. A feeling of safety and security washed over him. Soft kisses travelled over him, electric in their touch as they brushed his shoulders and neck. The exhilarating exhalation accompanied the ecstasy with each kiss and sent currents of elation coursing through him as they roamed to his ear.

"Find me," uttered, nay, demanded a whisper only a lover could conjure.

Will opened his eyes as fingers, gliding the curvature of his jaw, turned his head to see her beautiful complexion, pale against her dark eyes that drank him in with adoration. He was guided atop of her, and he admired her luscious lips and curly hair that spread on the pillow, like water splashes over rocks. He was entranced, hypnotized, and vulnerable as her fingers caressed the back of his neck, pulling him into her lips.

Will could feel her hand, feel her guiding, feel all of her as they undulated in euphoric rhythm. Her heels ran up the backs of his legs, pulling him in and binding him. Her hands clasped his back, gripping hard, pulling him into her. Her breathing laboured, chest heaving as her back arched, and she uttered a deep exotic sigh as they climaxed. She grasped a handful of his hair, pulling his head to the base of her neck. Her cheek pressed into his as their quivering bodies started to relax. Will pulled himself up on his elbows and looked down to behold her in her beauty.

Saraphima looked up with the same affection painted on her face, her fingers caressing his cheek. "Find me, Will."

Will awoke panting, saturated in sweat and gripping his pillow. The sheets were strewn on the floor. He sat up, rubbing his face and looked down at himself: viscous wetness was all over himself and the bed…

"Fuck me," he panted to himself between breaths and then came the utter realization that he, in fact, just did "fuck himself" in a sense. But her words rang in his mind, "find me." And he turned his gaze to the window, to the cemetery.

Will burst out the front doors, their hinges straining against the force. He rushed down the steps, the ring of keys clinking in his satchel as it reminding him of his purpose. The moon was eerie and nearly full, hovering in the sky as a luminescent eye that saw nothing and everything. It was obscured by wisps of clouds that glided by like an armada of haunting ghost ships. The wind had picked up since their retreat from the cemetery. Gravel in the drive crunched under his footfalls, the only thing that could be heard other than the low whooshing thrum that shook the treetops to and fro.

The darkness was heavy as he pushed his way into the carriage house, and he paused for a moment. Peering out from behind the tractor was the damaged front end of the Delta as if daring him to come closer. From his satchel, Will produced a torch, and with a *click,* he trained it on the car. A dark residual substance remained on the hood, but there was not near as much as there was before. The floor bore no such stain as though it had absorbed into the concrete. As the residual telekinetic energy had receded, so had the physical substance it left behind. He wanted to investigate; he wanted to get closer, but instead, he grasped the ring of keys they used to gain entry into the graveyard. As he hoisted the keys, Will noticed a crowbar hanging on the wall at the far end of the workbench. Hefting the tool, he mused that in old European folklore, iron was used to ward off evil spirits. It was hung at the threshold of an abode or around a pregnant woman, especially in childbirth, to keep the infant from being snatched up by fey folk or malicious spirits. *What could it hurt?* he thought to himself. It could help him pull up the tattered pieces of the gravestone from the grasses and dirt, and with the shit he'd seen, he felt a little safer holding it.

Richard awoke abruptly; the darkness in the room was dense and constricting save the moonlight that shone through the window. As he sat up, the bed was soggy, and he discovered that he was soaked. Water dripped from his body, and the sheets were saturated. He hastily turned to switch on the lamp but recoiled. Water was dripping from inside the lampshade. He threw back the covers; droplets shone as they caught the moonlight, sparkling tiny falling lights that disappeared into the darkness. Beads of water materialized on the floor, running up the walls and following the curvature of the crown moulding. The droplets travelled across the ceiling to rain down. It was now precipitating inside the room. His clothes were uncomfortably damp as Richard hastily dressed. A light flickered through the window. He paused to watch a figure with a torch move from where the carriage house was located in the direction of the cemetery.

"You've got to be joking," he uttered unamused, then he thought of their computers. The data! He grabbed the SLR film camera and directing it at his bed, he filled the room with its flash. The camera was wet, but it still worked. It was much better than the digital units that took the SD cards. Granted, it was more costly, and patience was indeed a virtue when it came to developing the film, but it would always prove to be far more reliable and not so easy to tamper with or doctor in the end. The room flashed brightly again, and again, then there she was.

Floating before him was the spectre of beauty and horror. Droplets fell through her translucent body that hovered in the air. Her clothes and hair glided weightlessly as though they were caught up in waving, rippling currents. Her eyes were lifeless yet aware as she looked down on him, displaying a modicum of consciousness. Her hands reached out as if to beckon for his own. Her expression was of sadness, a silent lament, gasping for air, trying to cry out, but there was only the silent sound of death.

Richard was overcome with sympathy and vulnerability as he reached for her, his fingers nearly touching hers before she vanished. The water in the room began to slow and thicken, appearing to ooze rather than freely flow. It now fell from the ceiling in long, thin, slimy tendrils. It began to percolate from the walls and slowly made its way to the floor in long viscous waves. Richard raised the camera, and the flash went off as he suddenly shuddered. He was gripped by a feeling of invasion and violation and collapsed to his knees, choking and gasping. Richard dropped the camera and clutched at his chest and throat. His eyes rolled to the back of his head as he crumpled in a paroxysm.

Will pushed himself against the tree, hunched over as if trying to protect himself from the deluge that had now penetrated his clothing. Rainwater ran down his flat hat, dripping from its ridge and traversing the curvature of his face as it made its way to his chin and dripped off. He felt like vomiting as he glared at the headstone he had looked at before and now finished assembling. His heart was in his throat, constricted, and it prevented him from swallowing. He looked away and then back again as if hoping the letters would change, hoping that it wasn't really true, but as he looked on, the name "Saraphima Gray" glared back at him. The stone words were haunting and harsh. They cut deep, and for the first time in a long time, Will could feel the stigma of a broken heart. It was familiar and painful, like getting cut by the same knife twice. The pain washed over him as he fell back against the tree with one knee up and the other leg straight out. His eyes refused to turn away. He looked on the forlorn stone the same way he did with Brynn, watching her withered self succumb to the reaper that was cancer, lost to all but memory. He looked on, allowing the same self-pity, same sadness, same anger to slowly overcome him, and he felt a loathing for the estate and his acceptance of this case.

Lightning flashed, and thunder clapped, reverberating through the wind. The trees shuddered, and an eerie shrill pierced the night. Will's head snapped in the direction of the raucous cry; he was looking at the third mausoleum. It was standing stoic and horrible in the darkness. The branches of large trees swayed in the wind, slightly distorting its features. Will wiped the wetness from the rain away from his eyes as he slowly rose to his feet, his eyes on the burial structure distorted from the aggressively swaying coniferous branches. The wind rushed past him, and the terrible harsh cry rang in his ears, this time from the darkness behind him. Will spun about. His heart was racing, his eyes wild with anticipating horror as he gazed out into the turbulent night, clutching the crowbar firmly with both hands.

Then he heard it, amidst the rushing furor of the wind, that same terrible gargling, hissing, churning cry from the carriage house. Amidst the fiercely swaying grasses, he could discern two eyes glistening from beyond the pitch of night. Will relinquished his grip on the crowbar with one hand and shone his torch into the blackness. Tombstones, poised like sentries in the field, peaked over the turbulent grasses while others spied through old tree branches that bobbed up and down in the wind. As Will lowered the torch, the glistening eyes returned, unblinking and terrible. They darted forward, moving violently and erratically, emitting a grotesque wailing as they jerked through the moving grasses. Will could see the broken woman from the carriage house pulling herself through the grasses. Her tattered limbs were flailing about as her body writhed, grotesquely twisting, lurching herself forward. Her cold, unblinking eyes fixed on him, and blood spilled from the corners of her mouth in long oozing rivulets

Will turned and faltered. A gasp of terror rushed from his lips as he felt her cold hand grasping his ankle, and he collapsed onto the broken headstone of Saraphima Gray. He cried out, feeling her terrible panting as she heaved herself atop of him. The horrific contortion of her body mixed with the grinding and popping of broken bones and joints. Her hand, grasping at the back of his head, turned his ear upward as she leaned over him, and her grisly churning croak mixed with a hideous whine. The coppery stench of blood flooded his senses as the rivulets dribbled onto his cheek and shoulder, and for the briefest of moments, Will thought she was trying to speak.

Driven by absolute fear or his will to survive, Will managed to roll himself over. Swinging the crowbar madly, he squeezed his eyes shut, and a series of dull thuds reverberated down the shaft of the crowbar. He paused, hearing only the storm, feeling only the rain. Will opened his eyes to see he had been striking the tree he had leaned on. Shaking, he wiped the wetness from his face again and staggered to his feet. He regained his composure and, with his torch, surveyed the darkness again for the entity.

Another shrill; he spun about, now facing the mausoleum once more. Standing before its metal door, was the same feminine spectre. Not as some dilapidated, broken thing with horrible unblinking eyes, but as a young woman with long flowing light-coloured hair, fair features, and a blood-and-dirt-smeared nightgown. She did not speak, but he could hear a whimpering on the bellowing air, a lament. Their eyes met, and Will felt a cold shudder course through his body, then the woman glided backwards, her eyes locked on his until she passed through the metal door into the mausoleum.

Will thrust the chisel of the crowbar between the metal door and the wooden jamb. Using the doorstop as a fulcrum, he heaved on the bar, utilizing its natural leverage. The stopper started to give under the force exerted, the jam cracking and splintering when the door abruptly shuddered. With a *click, clack,* he heard the workings of the old lock in motion. The tumblers fell in place, and the door was suddenly ajar. Will hesitated. He placed his hand on the cold metal door, and it swung open ostensibly of its own accord.

Lightning flashed again. It lit up the dark void before him. Shadows chased each other through the room as the lightning flashed for but a fraction of a second, and a ghostly young woman appeared in the eerie light, strewn about the floor screaming as the thunder roared. It barely drowned out her torturous lament. Will shuddered, stammering back and raising his forearm between himself and the ghastly presence as if to shield himself, and then she was gone.

Will paused for a moment, surveying the room with his torch. Fear surged through him. There was a heaviness in the air mingling with a pungent stench. The wind howled like a chorus of banshees in the night, and the door behind him slammed shut. Will whirled around, pressing himself against the cold metal barrier, pushing then pulling, but it refused to open. The notion of being trapped inside terrified him. Another clap of lighting illuminated the space beneath the door and flooded the small windows with its eerie light. Long peels of thunder rolled through the sky mixed with a woman's shrieks and protests, cries and sobs, pain and sorrow, and a pleading for release. Will covered his ears and fell to his knees, trying to cry out, wanting to command it all to stop, but he was stunned. The walls were spinning; he was careening through the room with wide, fear-filled eyes as if some horrific vertigo induced him. Then came a final blood-wrenching howl. Will found himself on his knees clutching at himself, stricken with pain that coursed through his body, weakened from hunger as though starving and dehydrated. Echoes of weak whimpering pleas for release reverberated around him then fell silent, leaving only the chorus of the thunderstorm. Will clutched at his chest, then his arms and legs. Everything was okay. No injuries. His breathing was laborious for moments as he regained his composure.

Suddenly, amidst the turmoil of the thunderstorm, there came a voice, a familiar voice that started as a whisper until it sounded as though Saraphima herself were standing behind him. Will froze as he listened to the voice speak, the very voice that belonged to that one person he so looked forward to seeing every time he ventured about this wretched estate.

"You've almost found me, Will," she said. "Isn't it beautiful, Will!" There seemed to be real emotion in her voice. "All of it, Will. So beautiful." There was a pause. "I'm waiting for you… can a ghost love, Mr. Stilton?"

At that, Will spun about to nothing, merely the darkness and the singular concrete coffin poised at the back wall of the mausoleum. He wasted no time and buried the crowbar under the coffin's lid. Shards chipped away as he aggressively heaved, scattering pieces to the floor about him. He broke the seal, allowing fresh air to rush in the void and release the stench of decay to permeate the room. Will faltered, reeling backwards with his free hand cupping his mouth and nose, stifling the urge to vomit.

With one final heave, Will pushed the heavy stone lid to the floor, training his torch to the contents of the coffin. He was not only taken by revulsion but by horror.

Two corpses glared back at him, one with hollow eyes and a slack jaw that smiled in that way skulls do, and the other but a corpse in the late stages of decomposition. The body was grotesquely broken and twisted, its jaw loose and tilted as if screaming with its teeth bared. It looked horrific with its long hair and dress caked and stained in the foul fluids of decay. Fetid pools collected in recesses, unable to drain away, impeded by the corpse beneath. Even with the ventilation, the cesspools of fluid, blackened and sickening, lay putrefying undisturbed. This must be the former vessel of that woman on the car, the very woman Richard had met before, the entity that grasped him only moments before, now glaring back at him with her haunting face. Will trained the torch on the inscription. The concrete coffin bore the name Ophelia Gray.

Saraphima's words rang out again, only now they were different. Will's attention turned to the door that abruptly swung open as though someone was bursting in. Will's heart raced. He stared hard at the threshold, gripping the crowbar, waiting for someone or something to reveal itself, but there was nothing. Saraphima's words rang out again. Only now he could hear her as though she were standing in the doorway. He trained his torch on the entrance to the mausoleum, but there was nobody. Will was frozen, gripped with both a horrific reluctance to see her and a desire to. He could not move but stayed poised by the opened coffin until her voice was clear in his ear.

"Come to me, Will."

It was as if she were standing right beside him, and he spun about, his heart still racing with excitement and consternation. But she was not there. Will turned back to the tortured and broken corpse. It was now sitting upright in the coffin; its head turned to face him, glaring at him with fetid, empty eye sockets. Its gruesome slack-jawed smile and what might have been her tongue lolling from a recess in her neck. Her nightgown, horribly discoloured, clung tightly to her degenerated body. Will shrieked in terror, "What the actual fuck!" as he stammered back and fled for the door.

He bolted from the crypt and through the cemetery as lightning cracked, thunder clapped, wind blew, and rain pelted. He paused at the gates and looked back. There, before the mausoleum, was the pretty woman in her blood-and-mud-smeared nightgown looking back, then she faded from sight. Will wasted no time. He darted through the gates and tore through the gardens towards the little cottage. He had to know. His heart wanted her to be there waiting. His head told him she was not of the living, and for the first time, he didn't want to believe it.

Will poised before the cottage. It was not as it had been the night he was here with Saraphima. He *was* here with her! She brought him here. Rainwater was trickling down his face, and his clothes were drenched and heavy, hanging off his body. Will wiped the intrusive wetness from his eyes. When he was here before, the cottage was alight and warm, inviting. Now it was dark and foreboding. Its exterior was a grimace that chased the world away. Darkness loomed through the windows, and not one bit of it seemed to beckon an invitation.

Structurally, it was very sound: nothing was falling off, and the painted board and batten was slightly peeling. The roof showed no signs of fatigue, and the chimney for the woodstove stood strong. Will paused in front of the door. He had to turn off everything he was and become the investigator he was known to be. A fearless and sceptical, no good investigator wanders about "hoping" beyond all measure to find "paranormal phenomena." No, the more you cannot disprove the existence, the more you make it a truth to yourself, the clients, and any other sceptic that would state otherwise… But he so wanted to believe. He wanted her to be on the other side of the door… He wanted her to be alive. With that one final thought, he pushed open the door. It squeaked as if to welcome him. The floorboards creaked and groaned as if familiar with his footfalls.

With each step, the floor announced his presence. What appeared forlorn from the exterior, though, dark and dank, was quite inviting in the interior. The light from his torch fluttered about the room as he inspected the cottage. He noted a thin layer of dust clung to the surfaces to suggest that the structure was not vacant long or that it still had a modicum of usage.

Lightning flashed in the window, drowning out his torch. Thunder rattled the roof, and shadows extended from every structure, every furnishing reaching and dancing all about him: another step, another groan. Will was beside himself. The other night when he was here, it was alive with an amazing atmosphere and energy. Blankets shrouded the furniture where he and Saraphima had sat and talked while sipping red wine. The love seat, the wing-backed chairs all veiled to appear as nothing more than drab blankets. A gust of wind whistled down the chimney pipe, and sooty air bellowed lightly from the wood stove, filling the room with the scent of burnt wood.

The familiar humming of a fridge was not to be heard, and the cupboards and cabinets had not been touched for some time. Will reached under a lampshade, the very lamp that he could see through the window when he first arrived with Saraphima the other night. He switched it on, and a soft glow emitted from beneath the lampshade, pushing back the darkness and adding a modicum of comfort as he slipped the torch in his jacket pocket.

"Hello, Mr. Will."

The voice came from his left. Will turned to meet the voice, but there was nobody there. Then, the sensation of a finger ran up the back of his neck and teased his wet hair. He turned again to meet Saraphima. She was real, so real.

"Welcome back to my home, Mr. Stilton."

He reached out to touch her, and she took his hand into hers.

"So warm," she said passionately as if drawing from some distant memory.

"So cold," Will replied, nearly stammering, choking on the words.

"This is turning out to be quite the pursuit for you," she said with a hint of enthusiasm and intrigue, running her finger across his jawline only to pause under his chin.

"Every day seems to be an adventure, lately," he replied as he would normally, trying to push aside the idea he just read her name on a headstone.

"You have found me." She smiled adoringly. "You came for me."

He could feel her hands gripping the back of his arms, her lips nearly kissing his chin as she spoke as if restraining a passion, then she stepped away smiling.

"You've found Alice." She smiled.

Will just looked at her. His thoughts drifted to the woman on the hood of the Delta, the entity that he and Richard had encountered. "I just uncovered two corpses in one casket."

She looked at him with agitation. "She was concealed in the very mausoleum that enshrines my mother. Stuffed in there like a bad secret."

Will just looked on, disgust mixing with horror on his face. "Ophelia Gray," he uttered, "is your mother."

Lightning flashed, and for the briefest of seconds, he thought Saraphima had turned translucent. In his mind, he knew what she was, but in this moment, he refused to believe it.

"How acute you are, Mr. Stilton." Her eyes flashed, alluring and spectral, as she looked hard at him.

Will's mind was racing, trying to assemble the pieces of a puzzle that would only come together of its own accord. "Who is Edgar, Saraphima…Who is he?"

Her eyes glowed with excitement at the mention of the name. For good or ill, Will could not tell, for as they flashed, expressions chased one another across her face.

"Be with me, Will," she said as she resumed the same adoring expression.

"What happened to you?" he queried as she drew closer.

Saraphima bound her arms around the back of his neck and drew herself in. Will was paralyzed with both fear and wonder as she drew in to his ear. "Mrs. Law happened."

She kissed his lips, cold yet soft, seemingly electric as she pressed herself into him, then drew back and laid her head against his chest. His heart thudded in his chest, threatening to break through, and his breath came in short gasps. He was frightened, but he was unsure if he was scared of letting go or scared of her.

"Be with me, Will. We can stay here, together."

Will's heart hurt; a pain in his chest combined with a lump in his throat, choking him. How he wished she was real. This all felt so real, but he knew better.

"Where is your mother?" Will's voice quivered slightly. He knew where her mother was physically, and it sent shivers down his spine. But he also knew by refusing to stay with Saraphima, he might incur some specific paranormal attention.

She drew back and looked at him with the same cocky grin she'd always had in the gardens. Her eyes adorned the same seductiveness they always had. "Why, Mr. Stilton, she is in my father's study with your brother."

Lighting, followed by thunder, filled the room with its eerily soft stroboscopic light. The lamp behind him stuttered then went out, diminishing what dim hue it emitted, and Saraphima was gone. He was now shrouded by the darkness of the cabin, and for a brief moment, he felt as though he had done the most terrible thing. Will felt like he'd just lost the one girl that could have made him happy, but he knew she was a perfect "intelligent haunt," as he would classify it, and for the first time, he didn't want to know.

Your emotions are a product of paranormal influence, he told himself, *nothing more.*

But they felt so real, and the hurt was a reality.

It is not any different than when someone abruptly loses their partner, their wife, their husband. The subjective reality is there to explain what the mind wants or perceives.

This was something that was all too familiar to him, and with that, he turned for the door but was pulled back by an unseen force, wrenching his arm.

Will's left hand, still clinging to the crowbar, now extended in front of him, and he was unable to move his appendage nor drop the crowbar. He was pulled again, and this time Will fell to the floor under the supernatural power. He desperately grasped at any object but came up empty as he was dragged through the cabin. His left hand was gripping the tool so hard it was turning white, and surges of cold energy rushed through his fingers and up his arm. He hollered out in agony. He could feel his arm freezing. His fingers felt as if they were going to shatter like frozen glass. Splinters in the floorboards and loosened nails caught at his coat as he was towed down a small hallway. He struck the wall so hard his left arm buckled, and the claw on the crowbar buried itself in his head, gouging just above his left temple.

Will lay motionless for a moment, then stirred, slowly hoisting himself to his feet. A droplet of blood fell to the floor, followed by two more. He hardly had time to regain his composure, to examine the extent of the injury on his head, when he was hurled into an open doorway, striking a bookshelf and falling to the floor. The bookshelf teetered over him, gently rocking, vacillating between wanting to stabilize itself and falling on top of him. As it pitched forward, a plethora of heavy books slid forward, adding to the momentum and solidifying its decision to fall. Will could hardly move out of the way. The bookshelf, with all of its contents, fell on him.

Will was agitated. He fumed, chanting a glut of maledictions as he was freeing himself from the pile of literature, pushing the bookshelf off. Amid his deluge of profanities, there came a *thud* as a small mass of books slid from the shelf and fell to the floor beside him. He paused for a moment, studying the collection of books that had not separated, slid apart, nor did their bindings fling open. Instead, they remained solidified in their union.

Now completely free and restraining from cursing out against Saraphima for fear that she might be lingering nearby, Will examined his left arm and hand. They were fine—a little numb from the trauma, but fine otherwise. Dabbing at the wound on his head with fluttering fingertips, Will concluded that it didn't seem too bad. There wasn't much in the way of pain.

Hell hath no fury like a woman scorned! he thought to himself, and as he drew back his hand, his fingertips were smudged with blood. *Bugger, that's gonna hurt later,* he added, and a sense of dread surged through him. *What would she'd have done if he agreed to be with her?* Suddenly, the beautiful young woman he'd grown fond of may not have been as innocent as he'd thought. Shuddering at the notion, he quickly pushed it out of his mind and turned his attention back to the unified stack of books. They were indeed fused together, and only some of the books had a title on the spine. *The Raven and the Rock, The Love Letter, The Cursed* and *I Hope You Like This Book.* As he read the titles aloud, he noticed there was an almost invisible seam that ran across the lot of them. Running his thumb along the seam, Will lifted the lid. It was a coffer, in the guise of books, as long as his forearm and deep enough to hide valuables. At first glance, anyone might write it off as a bunch of old hardcover literature. Will drew the torch from his coat pocket, and peering in the coffer, he saw many neatly folded pieces of paper; letters perhaps? They were all nicely folded, some in envelopes and pictures, but what captured his eye was a book. It bore a hasp and a pin that kept it closed.

Richard's going to get a kick out of this! he mused. *Oh, shit…Richard!* The sudden recollection of Saraphima telling him that his brother was with her deceased mother was enough to have a high sense of urgency flush over him. With the coffer under one arm, still carrying the crowbar, Will rushed back to the mansion that stood foreboding in the distance as the thunderstorm ravaged the sky like some looming ill portent of doom.

The front doors flew open, pulling Will with them. Gusts of wind bellowed in, and rain chased him into the foyer, dripping from his saturated clothes. He faltered in his footing and nearly fell before pushing the doors closed against the tide of rushing air and pelting droplets.

As he made his way up the stairs to their second floor, Will was suddenly aware of a thudding, some rhythmic hammering in a room down the very hall both he and his brother temporarily resided. As he rushed down the hallway, the thudding grew steadily louder and louder until he found himself before his door. It reverberated with whatever impact was occurring within.

Will entered the room. It was astonishingly cold. His heavy breaths were like wisps of clouds clinging to the air as they expanded and dissipated. The banging was horrendously loud. Richard was in the glider rocker, his eyes lolled to the back of his head, and he appeared to be staring into oblivion. The chair was rocking hard, pitching Richard back and forth as if wanting to launch his rigid body. Blood trickled from his nose and forehead from where he struck the bedpost. Both he and the rocker began to roll from side to side, and in a moment, Richard in the rocker was moving down the length of the room, adjacent to the bed. His head that held his rolled back eyes now hung to the side, teetering over his left shoulder, and he was humming a tune in some grotesque voice that was not his own.

Fright surged through Will as he looked on. The computers were strewn about the room, disconnected and distorted. Their monitors flashed and buzzed or displayed no life at all. Keys from the keyboards were torn away and scattered about, and Richard's headset was broken in two.

Richard trained his lolled back eyes on Will from his bent head. His neck looked unnaturally long as Richard's head wobbled on his shoulder. He then smiled a terrible grin; the possessing spirit was acknowledging Will's presence. The rocking abruptly stopped, and the glider rocker pivoted on the spot, scraping at the floor as if there were horrible claws beneath it. Now Richard was facing Will. His crooked neck popped and cracked as he began sitting upright, his back stiffening and his body rigid to the point where he appeared brittle. His blank eyes rolled down. His left eye was closely followed by the right. The pupils were so dilated the brown iris was seemingly nonexistent. He was staring at everything and focusing on nothing, glaring like the open eyes of a corpse. As Will made his way across the room, Richard's left eye snapped into focus and stared at Will, egregious and heinous as it fixated on him. The glider rocker turned on the spot, scratching at the floor with those horrible claws that sounded as though they were beneath it, only stopping when Will did. Now both of Richard's eyes were focused on him.

"Look at her, my love." Richard held up his arms as though he were cradling a babe close to his chest. "Look at her. Isn't she beautiful? So beautiful," he croaked in his most unnatural voice that sent shivers surging through Will.

In Richard's arms was a pile of neatly tied envelopes wrapped in a small blanket. They exhibited the unique appearance of something that had yellowed over time.

Will's attention then turned to where the glider rocker had been stationed. He manoeuvred past his brother. The chair was deathly cold, and he felt as though shocks of energy were coursing through his body, pushing him away every time he grasped for it. Richard merely looked on adoringly at the neatly bundled envelopes he so gently cradled. Will could not help but notice as he passed by that the blanket could be perceived as a receiving blanket.

Within moments, he found himself peering into an elusive hiding space, kept secret by the hinged inner panel of the wainscotting and hidden behind the glider rocker. How had he not noticed it before? Will glanced at Richard, who was still occupied, swaddling the envelopes. Reaching in, he removed another bundle of envelopes, neatly tied and wrapped in cloth. Behind him, Richard started humming again in that grotesque tone. Will surveyed the door; there was nothing to grasp. Running his fingers on the panel's edge looking or some "hidden switch," the door rolled back with a *click,* then came forward, firmly closing in place with a *clack.* It must have a spring mechanism in it! It was hidden in plain sight, and even with the horrible grooves the rocker had left in the floor, he never would have noticed anything, nor anyone else for that matter. Will then turned to Richard, who had ceased his foul humming and was fixated on him with those eyes and twisted smile.

Will could feel the terror welling up within him as he looked at Richard in this horrific state. Richard was sitting before him, but it wasn't his brother with that twisted grin and those horrible eyes. He wanted to call out to his brother, but he could not form the words. A fear for his brother washed over him, and for the first time in a long time, he didn't know what to do.

"Isn't she just adorable?" exclaimed Richard, coddling the neatly tied envelopes swaddled in the blanket.

Will looked on for a moment. He wanted to grasp the envelopes, but he was too hesitant. He did not know how his brother would react to his intrusion.

"She is beautiful, Richard," he said, choking back terrifying anxiety.

Richard stiffened, his smile converted to a grimace, and he scowled at Will. A terrified Will felt himself shrinking in the corner of the room under the horrific gaze.

"Not Richard… Saraphima! Our daughter, our beautiful daughter." His voice croaked with resentment as he scolded Will.

Will's fear quickly turned to animosity for the invading spirit, and he walked over to the scotch bottle, uncapped it, and took a long, satisfying swig. It was already burning and warming his chest before he pulled the bottle away. He looked at Richard and knew what he was going to do. He hoisted the bottle again, then slammed the bottle on the table and marched over to his brother. Grasping Richard by his broad shoulders, Will shook him aggressively. *C'mon Richard. I know you're in there!* He cried out as he did so, "Let him go, you dead, dodgy fucking git!" Richard glared at Will menacingly, and an ugly hissing emanated from behind clenched teeth, but it only fueled Will's anger, and with an open palm, Will slapped him as hard as he could.

Richard was nearly hurled from the chair. His head violently jerked to one side from the blow, and his body shuddered.

Will's hand instantly stung. It pulsed through his fingers, working its way up his forearm as he slapped him again. Will cocked his arm back for a third time but halted as Richard called out, clenching his jaw and cradling his cheek, trying to shield himself from another blow. Will lowered his hand, his anxiety settling, and he relaxed and sighed with relief.

Richard looked up at him, an expression of confusion and anger spreading across his face as he cradled his face and jaw in his hands. The envelopes and blanket spilled on the floor. "What the bloody hell!" he hollered. Anger flashed in his eyes, but Will felt nothing but relief.

Richard dabbed at his forehead and face, trying to reassure himself that everything was okay. Neither one of them had seen this before, nor had they experienced anything of the like.

Will grabbed the bottle, leaned against the table under the window, and took a moment to compose himself, watching as Richard suddenly realized the computers were strewn about chaotically, taking in their flickering screens and broken keyboards. One laptop's display assembly had been torn from the keyboard, the keys scattered about the room, and his earpiece broken in half.

"What in the name of all that is holy happened!?" Richard sprang from the chair and rushed to the aid of his computers, cursing at the parts scattered about the room.

"Are you aware of what just took place?" asked Will calmly, a modicum of concern lingering in his voice.

Richard took a moment then turned to face his brother. "Yeah, you bloody hit me! Fucking tosser!" Then he gestured for the scotch.

"There is not much left," Will exclaimed as he handed the bottle to his brother.

"I'm sure there is a stash of liqueur in this place," Richard said as he brought the bottle to his lips.

Will had lost any kind of ethics. He cared not if he violated Mrs. Law's stash of booze. Never before had either one of them drank this much on a case, if at all. Will was known to bring a bottle or a flask, but they always departed, having imbibed only a little.

"There is a first aid kit in the van," said Richard, looking at the gouge in Will's head. He handed back the bottle, which had a little more than a quarter left.

"You better take a look in a mirror." Will laughed as he took the bottle. "You just got your ass kicked by a ghost!"

Richard's head hurt. The pain was pounding but not overwhelming, like a vice lightly gripping his head, putting more tension on the sensitive tissues. He pretended he didn't hear his brother and his mockery and continued with assembling his computers.

"Tell me, Will, what did happen?" he asked as he worked, not lifting his eyes but bent on listening. He wanted to hear it, but he didn't want to accept it. Richard knew what just took place. For some reason, it felt more like a nightmare, but he knew better. His body was fatigued; he could feel it.

His limbs were weak, and he felt as though his energy had been depleted. He wanted nothing more than to lie under his covers and deal with whatever the morning may bring.

Will stood in a moment of silence, watching Richard set everything up, connecting to the cameras they had placed about the property. One by one, they popped up on the screens, and the brothers could see what the eyes of the cameras saw.

Will wanted to confirm what Richard had stated in his possession. He wasn't sure if he'd remembered what he had called the little bundle of papers in the swaddling cloth. He wanted to tell him that her name was on the headstone, Saraphima Gray, and that he met her in her cabin. If he told anybody, he wanted to tell his brother that the woman he adored was a ghost. A *ghost*! The very word crippled his mind with questions and feelings! He had been conversing with a ghost all this time and had not known. This was that story one could tell and be branded as crazy or suffering from post-traumatic stress disorder. But how could he? The words refused to form; they lingered on his tongue, refusing to come out, defying his will to speak them as though it was forbidden or something was denying him the ability.

After a moment, Will told of his encounter with the "broken woman" and how he found the corpses in the coffins: the mangled body that must be the very woman from the hood of the car.

"It was the woman from the other night on the road," verified Richard, clutching his chest.

"Does it hurt?" asked Will.

"It tingles from time to time... a pins and needles feeling," his brother replied as he finished assembling two of his computers. He sighed with relief as he leaned back against the bed, now examining his broken earpiece. His gaze turned to Will, letting him know that he was, in fact, listening.

Will continued, "The corpse entombed in the locked mausoleum, her name was Ophelia Gray. Every other one bore the Law name."

"I'm telling you, brother. There is something utterly shady going on here. You should've seen it! Who stuffs a corpse in a coffin like that? An unscrupulous, murderous twat! I'll wager they're hiding something." Will took a moment as if waiting for a distraction. He looked at the door, half expecting Lucy to come barging in, then to his brother. The image of Richard's face was forever imprinted in his mind. The whites of his eyes turned towards the back of his skull. His face twisted unnaturally by what had taken him and that terrible hissing that was not his own. The worst was how utterly helpless he felt in that moment, a feeling he wished never to experience again.

Though Richard's expression hadn't changed, his eyes seemed almost distant as Will told of how he found him, how he was possessed, coddling envelopes as though they were a child.

"Your face wasn't even yours. Your voice was not bloody human," Will exclaimed. His face twisted, and he recoiled as though the very thought would forever haunt him.

He was also pretty sure his brother took a modicum of pleasure in the retelling of how he struck him, twice no less.

"Best exorcism ever!" concluded Will. He paused with a smug, victorious smile, then proceeded to pick up the envelopes and bundle them with the ones he pulled from the wall. Will placed the coffer on the table under the window and, hoisting the crowbar, told how he received the gash on his head and how the supernatural forces had pulled him down the hall and into a bookshelf where he'd found this coffer.

Will paused time and time again during the regaling of his story, trying not to say Saraphima's name. *But why? Why was it so hard to tell his own brother how the woman he had been seeing all over this estate was ethereal? Admittedly, maybe he didn't want to accept it?*

Richard regarded his brother, reading him. He wasn't a fool. He was, however, not only the technologically savvy one between the two, but he was also the more counter-intuitive and knew Will better than Will knew himself at times. This was one of those times, mere moments, and in those moments, Richard absorbed a wealth.

He could have said anything, but he chose not to. Instead, he studied his brother intently. Will was not one to hide something, quite the opposite, in fact. If something needed to be said, half the time, it was Will saying it and how well it was received was dependent on his mood. No, Richard studied his brother for a moment longer. "Open it up!" he exclaimed, bringing his brother and his mind back into the room.

Opening the coffer, Will gently spilled its contents onto the table. Richard's face lit up when he saw the little book with the hasp, but Will quickly snatched it up and removed the pin, eager to delve into its secrets.

Richard began sifting through the neatly folded papers. One, in particular, was of a heavier stock, which immediately grabbed his attention. His own eyes widened. "Bugger me!" he exclaimed as his eyes traversed to the will he held before him. He looked over to his brother, who was paying no attention to him. However, he was completely invested in this book. Turning his attention back to the will, he saw it bore a legal seal and a multitude of signatures: Mr. Edgar Law, Saraphima Gray, and Nathan Williams from Williams Brother's Legal Firm in Brakenstone, UK—the lawyer and the witness. The will bequeathed the entirety of the Law estate to the recipient/survivor, Saraphima Gray. "Bugger me sideways," he uttered again. He thought of what the drunkard, Pete, had mentioned back in the tavern, how Mrs. Law had apparently axed her own husband. He couldn't think of a finer motive than this will. He sifted through the neatly folded papers, and gently opening them up, he found they were nicely written letters addressed to "Dearest daughter" and ending with "loving father, Edgar."

Will was completely invested in the little book, Saraphima's diary. It was something real, tangible, a gateway into her world beyond the vale and obscurities of the paranormal. He was reading her very handwriting, and it was not, all of it, good. She'd written of her secrets, emotions, and fears. The only thing she could confide in was her father and this little book he held. It was filled with passages of moments spent with her father, glorious treasured times, and feelings of longing for her mother, her memory so distant now, and of how she still missed her dearly. It spoke of dread for her estranged, loathsome stepmother, Eleanor Law. Who, according to the passages, hated her very existence. In her words, there was genuine fear of the stepmother, who looked at her as though she were plotting her very demise. There were even accusatory thoughts of Mrs. Law being the root of her mother's demise and how she cared not for the lilies Saraphima had planted around the fountain in remembrance of her mother, Ophelia Gray.

CHAPTER ELEVEN

FAMILY BLOOD

The following morning, Will had risen early or had hardly slept. Either way, his body exhibited all the features of tiredness, stress, and a festering loathing for his employer. It was almost as if he had come to terms with the case, a sense of closure, but fragments of anger remained, and resentment toward Mrs. Law grew.

The side of his head was bandaged with a dressing from the first aid kit he and Richard had retrieved from the van. In their travels from room to automobile, they stumbled upon a lavishly decorated cabinet that held varieties of whiskeys and brandies. Will wrote it off as an "overdue expense" while Richard referred to it as "stress relief."

On the table, he had placed a recorder. Any other day it would have been known as an electronic voice recorder, utilized to gather electric voice phenomena. But today, it was simply a regular recorder. He sipped his morning coffee. It was perfect. He relished the taste and the aroma. It just felt like the perfect start to this day. The cook soon came in with breakfast: muffins, crepes, French toast, all coated with icing sugar and strawberries for that proverbial perfect presentation.

Richard soon came in. He strode over to one of the tapestries, fastened a small object to its frame, and hastily walked out, then returned moments later. "Everything is in place, and the connection is perfect," he said in a low voice as though he didn't want the murals to overhear. Richard had bandages bound about his head, and his nose wasn't any worse for wear, but Will could almost make out the telltale shadows shrouding his eyes, the beginnings of perhaps moderate black eyes. It would be easy to surmise that neither one knew what they were doing or mayhap had been drinking while trying to bandage one another, and quite honestly, they would not be wrong.

After some time, Mrs. Law entered the room with Lucy in tow. She had her hair pulled back tightly in a bun and wore a fitted black shirt that had purple accents and a high pleated collar. It fastened at the end of her sleeves. Her blouse tapered to her skirt, which was pleated at the waist and draped loosely, allowing for her full stride. She said nothing as she ventured to the end of the table, nor did she acknowledge their presence. Her eyes were ever forward as though she had purpose, and only when she turned to face Will and Richard did her expression fall from sternness to disgust. Lucy, however, glared at the duo the minute she walked in with wide eyes, nearly forgetting to pour Mrs. Law her morning coffee.

"What the bloody hell is this?" she exclaimed, her wide angry eyes darting between the two. "Messrs. Stilton, I do not entirely know what you are playing at, but if you insist on injuring yourselves on my property, I would like to inform you that I will not be held responsible for your idiocy or your shenanigans."

She regarded the two invalids for a moment. "Tell me, Messrs. Stilton, how does a team of paranormal investigators hurt themselves to the degree you appear to be hurt?" She glared at them hard, and her gaze was foul. For once, Lucy did not share her expression or attitude. She avoided the gaze of the two brothers, trying not to fidget with her hands to advertise her discomfort. Instead, she simply remained subordinate to her employer and dared not speak.

Mrs. Law continued. "You cannot provide the service I employed you for, and now you dare to show yourselves to me as though you had been beaten, by what around here? You have hardly spoken to the workers, and every day is one disappointment after another. I feel I have gravely misplaced my trust and funds."

"Actually, Mrs. Law," Will chimed in. "We have done exactly what we were procured to do."

She scowled at him, but he calmly continued. "You hired our services to investigate the presence of the paranormal within your estate, and we have done just that. In fact, we've seen shite here that'll turn you, how shall I say, Gray." He was looking at her almost defiantly. "It was you who told me that you'd be the biggest sceptic I had ever seen, and you have been true to your words." Will was holding his composure quite well. His mood changed, somewhat for the better, as they had sifted through the envelopes and reviewed the contents of the coffer the previous night. He had discussed with Richard the bigger issues at play, and none of it was good. In fact, this case was far fouler than just a simple haunting. And Mrs. Law's refusal to cooperate with the people she hired demonstrated the presence of vile secrets she nor Lucy were willing to reveal.

Will remained stoic and spoke calmly, with a half-smile. "Is it alright if we leave this recorder here for now?" He pointed to the recorder on the table and glanced at Richard, who couldn't suppress a smile. His brother casually ate his breakfast, clearly taking a modicum of delight watching the plethora of expressions flutter across both ladies' faces.

Mrs. Law looked at the tiny device. "I care not for your little toys and trinkets, Mr. Stilton. They have not proven to provide any evidence, and they have failed to impress me."

Will noted her lack of acknowledgment with a raised eyebrow.

Richard bent and grabbed his digital camera out of his camera bag and, brandishing it, said, "We have something to show you. This was taken yesterday, then another one last night."

Mrs. Law looked coolly down her nose at him, then cast her eyes to the side. "I told you, I am not taken by your little toys, Mr. Stilton."

Will chimed in. "We're showing you via camera because one cannot alter the photograph on the unit before it is downloaded to a computer. We're simply eliminating that doubt that so vividly lingers in your mind."

Mrs. Law regarded him as though he were some mischievous sleuth. "Very clever, Mr. Stilton, and very well, let us see these pictures you have for me."

After putting on her glasses, she peered at the screen of the camera, at the translucent, twisted body of a woman. Her eyes flicked over the camera screen, at the hood of the Delta and what was sprawled on the hood. Will watched as the blood ran from her face. With the press of a button, the picture vanished and was replaced by another. Now she was looking at the spectre of a woman in Richard's bedroom, her hair and clothes waving in the air as though she were weightless, floating in the water, her face straining as if she were gasping for air.

"I took this picture right before I was possessed by the spectre that did this number on my face," said Richard with a bit of resentment and agitation as he gently removed the bandages from his head, revealing the wounds from the previous night.

Will gained a small sense of satisfaction as he watched on. Now Mrs. Law appeared as though she had been completely exsanguinated.

She stepped back. Her face had contorted into a horrific expression as she glared at the two men. "What are these? What are they, and how dare you present to me these horrid depictions?" she demanded, her eyes glaring at Richard. "I do not know how you did that, but clearly, I am no fool. No, the fools here are the two of you, trying to shock me into believing what you want to find in this place."

Will raised his voice slightly as he became stern. "We were procured by you to investigate the Law estate for the presence of paranormal phenomena in the hopes, by you, that in my sceptical approach to proving it, I would, in fact, disprove it." As Will spoke, he and his brother could see her agitation beginning to apex.

"We have done our job. Our values are not misplaced, Mrs. Law." Richard placed the camera on the table and pulled an envelope out of his camera bag as Will pulled one out of his inner jacket pocket.

Mrs. Law trained her glare on Will as she continued, "I will not have it, Mr. Stilton. The only thing haunting this place is your corrupt minds. Not once have you brought me any kind of evidence that I have requested. Your services have been proven futile and false, and my estate is going to flounder because of your incompetency. Consider your services, or lack thereof, terminated Messrs. Stilton, and I expect your departure by the end of the day."

"Tell me about Saraphima," Will demanded as he dropped the old envelopes and a small diary on the table, meeting Mrs. Law's gaze. Will's eyes stared intently with an energy and a type of madness he could not hide. It transformed his face and washed over his eyes. He suspected it wasn't a good idea to blatantly take on Mrs. Law. There was most likely a more tactical and amicable approach, but he was beyond caring and way beyond any kind of politics.

Mrs. Law's head snapped up from the envelopes on the table to stare at Will. For a moment, she looked lost, absent in thought as though she hadn't heard that name for a long time.

"Saraphima?" She repeated the name as a question but did not dare drop her composure. She still stood proudly.

"Yes, Mrs. Law, Saraphima Gray... And Ophelia Gray while we're at it." Will could see the rage welling up inside of her ashen colour, returning with vigour. Her face was now red, and her hands trembled with rage.

"Edgar was your husband, Mrs. Law?" Will was now brandishing the printed photographs before the two women. "And you knew he was having an affair with Ophelia Gray."

At that moment, he placed photographs on the table for all to see. They were washed with age but ever as visible as the day they were taken. One showed a woman in the very glider rocker in Will's room, and in her lap, she coddled an infant. The other was a portrait of Edgar, Ophelia, and Saraphima, who looked to be in her thirties. Last was a photograph of the three of them: Edgar, Ophelia, and Saraphima, all in their best dress.

"Where were you in all of this, Mrs. Law? And how does Alice fit into all of... this..." Will's gesture was toward Mrs. Law and the entirety of the estate. "It's safe to assume she was in your employ before her demise?"

She grasped at the pictures, but Richard was quick to snatch them up, giving her a cocky smile.

"Those are not yours to take, you behemoth!" Mrs. Law's words were vile as they came from clenched teeth.

"Nor were they ever yours!" he retorted, biting into a muffin.

Will held up a cluster of love letters written so neatly, a correspondence confessing mutual devotion and lust. "None of these love letters state your name. As a matter of fact, there is tremendous mention of undying love, inheritance, and legacy between Edgar and Ophelia. But not once does it mention your name."

Confusion played on Mrs. Law's face, along with the anger as her eyes darted between the two brothers. "How did you come across this? How dare you fabricate such lies, foul the memory of my Edgar!"

Richard stood now. "The gravestones of Edgar Law and Saraphima Gray have been smashed."

She now glared at him with the same hatred she bore for Will. "You dare to invade the sanctity of our family plot? You're both vile."

Richard simply smiled. "The only vile person here is the one who desecrated those gravestones."

"Your husband was with someone else: Ophelia Gray." Will's voice was accusing and harsh. "They had a daughter, Saraphima Gray. How detrimental that must have been for you, considering how you two never had children of your own. So tell me, Mrs. Law, how is it that your husband, his lover, and their daughter are all in your family cemetery, and yet here you are? How has this not been suspicious before?"

Mrs. Law stiffened, regaining some of her composure and regal stance. She looked down her nose at the two miscreants accusing her.

"You really are pathetic, Mr. Stilton. Your accusations are unfounded and insulting. You are merely fabricating a theory you simply cannot solve and using my deceased family, no less. Nothing more than conniving heathens. How dare you? You know nothing!"

"What is going on here, Mrs. Law," asked Will calmly.

Mrs. Law glared at Will and Richard a long moment before announcing, "You have much to prepare in readying yourself for your departure. I suggest you get to it." And she and Lucy turned for the door almost in unison. Lucy, who exhibited a grave expression on her face, looked at the duo, then to the ground as she started to follow.

"What happened here, Lucy?" asked Richard almost sympathetically, but Mrs. Law was quick to shut him down.

She spun around with hatred in her glare. "You don't speak to her; you speak to me."

She then turned her threatening gaze to Lucy. "I forbid you to speak to these miscreants, if you know where your loyalties lie."

Lucy merely nodded and fell in line behind her.

"There is more than just a haunting here, Mrs. Law. There is murder and deception," Will shouted after her.

She paid him no mind as she reached for the door handle.

"You stood to lose everything. That is why you killed your husband, Edgar. You killed his mistress, Ophelia, and you killed their daughter, Saraphima, who stood to inherit this estate upon his death. And you killed Alice, who knew everything, who fled from here, and you ran her down with your Delta."

Mrs. Law halted, her hand on the door handle. "You should be very careful how you choose your words, Mr.

Stilton. They may end up costing you more than you are willing to give."

"Is that a threat, Mrs. Law?" Will replied with the same cool tone.

"Advice, you loathsome creature, advice to live by. Merely accusations. You have nothing." She was now looking directly at him again, no doubt regarding him as nothing more than a pathetic spinster of tales.

"We have a Last Will & Testament from Edgar, willing Saraphima the estate in its entirety. I have seen the body of Alice crammed in the tomb of Ophelia. And as outlandish as it sounds, I have spoken with the gardener Saraphima herself." Will slapped his hand on the table.

"Spoken, you say?" The words ran off her tongue in the most condescending tone. "We haven't had a gardener since Saraphima tragically passed away. We merely employ some of the workers in the orchard or from the vineyard to work in the gardens."

Richard's eyes flicked to Will, and although his demeanour didn't change, Will could sense the surprise his brother was stifling.

"Now I know you are as crazy as you are useless, Mr. Stilton, you and your brother. With such blatant accusations such as these, it's a wonder why I am not motivated to come after your little company. The media these days, Mr. Stilton, is powerful, especially if you have the money."

She turned for the door, pausing to give Will a grave look over her shoulder. "Which I have, Mr. Stilton. Can you say the same?" Then she disappeared.

Lucy hesitated for the briefest of moments but quickly fell in her place behind Mrs. Law.

A satisfaction welled up in Will, but at the same time, it wasn't satisfying.

"Your gardener woman is… were you ever going to tell me, Will?" Richard fumed.

Will just looked at Richard then sipped his coffee. He was uncomfortable with the very notion of keeping things from his own brother, but this just felt personal, even though it was still business—their business.

"I'm sorry, Richard. It was a little personal and somewhat intrusive. Sit down, and I will tell you everything that happened. I promise you will understand." Will kept his tone sympathetic but direct as he gestured to the chair.

Richard sat down. His normal, happy morning demeanour seemed reduced to a bland expression of scepticism and resentment, but Will understood, and soon, so would his brother.

CHAPTER TWELVE

WICKEDNESS

Will was not one for pleading, nor was he one for monomania, especially in his field of expertise and most certainly not one for drama, but the very outset of this day was a triumvirate of them all. After Mrs. Law stormed out with what appeared to be a distraught Lucy in tow, he shared his experiences with Richard. Thankfully he understood his brother was no fool, and his eyes were keen. He seemed to have seen Will wandering off more than once.

"You are a great many things, brother, but one thing you and I are not is stupid and unobservant. You've been dropping tell tales whether you realize it or not. You've been as distracted as you have been focused and quite honestly, never have I seen you like this."

They sat in silence for a moment. Will felt like he needed a dunce cap and a corner, but what he craved was a nip and another coffee. Even though the whole job was an absolute failure in Mrs. Laws's eyes, he, along with his brother, was walking away with experiences no other paranormal investigator he knew of could boast about. Even the university and privately funded firms and institutes hadn't reported such happenings in their scientific journals on the topics.

The mark on Richard's chest was nearly faded, but they had the photographic evidence to back it up. The woman on the hood of the car, the woman in the fountain, the woman floating in the room. Heck! He even performed some backward dilapidated version of an exorcism that nobody credible was likely to believe.

"I oughta cuff you right here! That would make me feel better for sure!" Richard said.

Before Will could respond, before he could even object, a sturdy jab struck his cheek. Everything stopped. The world froze, and his mind went blank as the force of the blow reverberated through his body, and he stumbled backwards into a chair, which flipped him, tipping the chair on its side. He sat dumbfounded on his back with his legs draped over it.

"What the bloody hell?" he called out to Richard, looking about the room as though he were trying to locate his senses.

"Now we're square," he heard his brother exclaim as he suddenly came into focus, standing over him with outreached hands.

"We were never unsettled, you freaking behemoth," scolded Will as he grasped Richard's hand and was hoisted to his feet.

"I feel better for it," Richard replied with a smile.

They pushed their way through the front doors, Richard eager to bear witness to the claims his brother hurled at a stoic Mrs. Law. "I'm telling you, Richard, they stuffed that poor woman in a coffin after running her down, and they killed Ophelia and made her death an accidental drowning in the fountain," exclaimed Will, still rubbing his cheek as they descended the stairs.

Richard looked back at the fountain as they marched past the gardens toward the cemetery. He thought of the photograph, the same lady that was floating in his room. What Richard had not noticed was the feminine silhouette hovering in one of the windows that overlooked the estate. Obscured by the curtains, she hid behind as she watched the duo walk past the carriage house and disappear behind the overgrown foliage to the gates of the family graveyard.

The door to the crypt was still unlocked. It creaked slightly as Will pushed it open, letting in the light of day that reached in with its warm glow to illuminate the still-open tomb. Richard could already see the limbs of the tattered corpse over its edges. Her skin was in such advanced stages of decomposition without her being properly embalmed, and she reeked of decay which now quickened in the fresh air. After all that they had seen, he had not put it past the corpse to hurl itself from its resting place. As he looked on her face, her broken jaw, the same hisses he heard that night came rushing back to him, and he cringed with fear. Beneath her, lying eerily sombre, was Ophelia, her eyes shut but her jaw open. She seemed to protest the presence of Alice so crudely stuffed in her resting place. He looked at Will, who looked up at him.

"We're over our heads, Richard," he said. "I want to solve this, but by the same token, I want to get out of here in the worst way."

Richard stepped away from the tomb. "We have our ticket out of here. We've been fired from the case, Will. We can go home and continue with our lives as though none of this had happened. Just another cold case where we come out a little wiser."

"I want to concur, proclaim my agreement out loud and peel out of this place, not daring to look back, but I have to know—how did Mr. Law and Saraphima die then?" asked Will.

As much as Will wanted to debunk the conundrum surrounding the demise of Saraphima and Edgar, he also wanted to put Saraphima to rest. Sometimes the worst things in life are the best things; one just cannot always see it until the end.

A shadow fell against the wall, obstructing the daylight and from it came a familiar voice. Richard spun about to see Lucy standing in the doorway brandishing a revolver. It was older in appearance and looked heavy, for she held it with two hands as she directed it at them.

"I would never have thought desecrating graves would be so becoming of you, Messrs. Stilton," she said in a nearly resentful tone. "I helped you in the hopes that you would make your departure sooner. Never had I thought you would go to such lengths as breaking into crypts and opening tombs. Where else have the two of you been that I may correct anything you could have tampered with, remedy anything you may have exposed? Now, let's see those hands of yours."

Richard was facing her now, along with his brother. Their hands were up, palms forward, shoulder height.

"So this was all you, this whole time," said Richard.

Lucy merely smiled. "We are all guilty of something, Mr. Stilton. I can only imagine what skeletons the two of you must harbour in your closets." With that, she gave Richard a taste of his own, with a wink and a smile.

"So, Mrs. Law has nothing to do with this? That would explain why she is so cynical of us and refuses to acknowledge anything," said Will.

Lucy scoffed at the notion. "There is more to Eleanor Law than the likes of you could ever comprehend. I am not to be underestimated, Messrs. Stilton, but Eleanor is the one you should be afraid of. I like to consider myself a little more forgiving than she. But, since we find ourselves in this debacle, and I have the upper hand, I feel that I can at least divulge to you that Mrs. Law means everything to me. She has given me more than I could ever hope to reciprocate, plucking me from the streets of despair as a young woman. She gave me this place and her kindness. She liberated me from what could have been an utterly dismal life, and I have become utterly passionate about my loyalties to her.

"But I think the two of you should stay a little longer, at least until I can figure out what to do with you. So you just sit tight, and I will be back when I can." With her pistol trained on them, she produced a key from her pocket and hastily closed one door, then reached for the other.

Richard quickly reacted. He lunged forward, throwing himself into the closing door with all of his weight. The thin metal door buckled and bulged, and the hinges creaked and snapped as the door collapsed under his weight. There was a moment of resistance as it struck Lucy. She bellowed in pain, and the two tumbled down the concrete steps. Will was behind them. He emerged to see his brother in the grass, hoisting himself up, but there was no Lucy. Blood trickled down the door and smeared the concrete where she fell, but she was nowhere to be seen.

"Now can we leave?" asked Richard, still a little dazed as Will helped him up.

"Now we can leave," replied Will. "Screw this place, but all of our gear is in our rooms. We need to get in and get out. Grab what is important and book it."

Richard nodded in agreement. "I don't think it would be wise to seek out Mrs. Law just yet."

"Agreed, she may very well have a larger role in this than Lucy let on," Will replied. Richard cut across the lawn, briskly moving past the crypts with his brother beside him. They were almost to the gates when *pow,* a bullet whizzed past them, striking the stone column that held the gate. Foliage and bits of stone exploded into the air. Richard spun about instinctively to see where the discharge came from.

There was Lucy, emerging from behind one of the crypts, her lips and chin a bloody mess as the fluid ran from her nose and dripped onto the bust of her dress. *Pow.* She fired again. Sparks flew from the gate, and a reverberance from the old iron rang out. Richard and his brother were now in a full run, dodging a report from the revolver. There came a whizzing as the bullet disrupted the air between them, striking the gate again. They managed to flee from the graveyard, Richard uncertain how far behind them Lucy was.

"Follow me," hollered Will, overtaking his brother as they fled into the gardens. He turned down a trail, and within moments, they were at the door of the cottage. He pushed his way through the door and ducked from sight beneath the view of the windows, motioning for Richard to take cover. The atmosphere was a little heavier, and the scent was familiar. Will didn't think he would ever be back, or at least not this soon.

"I don't see her," uttered Richard as he peered through one of the windows, trying to keep his distance from the glass. "Maybe she went back to the mansion?"

"Maybe. She could still be in the cemetery for all we know," Will said, also peering through one of the windows. "We need to make it to our rooms and to the van. We need to get the hell out of here." He looked at Richard, who was looking back.

"I'm done with this place." Richard smiled. "Fuck the lot of 'em?"

Will simply nodded with the hint of a smile.

Richard peered through the window once again. "Nothing," was all he said, his eyes scanning the outside through the glass.

Will relaxed slightly, but his mind was racing; the two sat silent for a moment. Nothing. There was nothing to be heard beyond the walls of the cabin, but Will knew that a gun-wielding Lucy was out there on the hunt.

"It's only a matter of time before she comes here," said Will, now sitting with his back to the wall, his eyes looking about the room for anything that could be used in his favour, but his thoughts were taken to Saraphima.

"This was her place," he said, "Saraphima's," Will spoke as though he had forgotten their current debacle as if he recalled some distant memory.

Richard turned from the window and, copying his brother's sitting posture, looked on, listening.

Will continued, "I reckon it was her mother's place too, but that would be doubtful. They had two separate roles in this forsaken place."

Richard's expression softened. "I feel for you, Will. I really do, but you need to get your head straight if we're to get out of here alive." He rose and extended his hand to help his brother up, and in that very moment, time seemed to stall.

Will felt paralyzed as he watched a beautiful Saraphima emerge from the hall in an alluring sundress. Her hair bounced in its short curly locks, her eyes were trained on him, and her smile was bright. Her bust was pushed up, accentuating her luscious breasts, and her figure was stunning. The dress swayed with her hips in such a fluid motion, and Will was completely enchanted as she walked over to him. Her hands were cold as they cupped his jaw and chin, raising his head slightly. Her lips were chilled as they kissed his forehead. He could feel their texture, the loving caress, as she pulled away and stood back. Then her smile faded, and she lifted both her hands toward Richard, outstretched and clasped together as if they were a pistol.

Will's eyes widened. Fear and action overcame him simultaneously as he reacted, rolling toward his brother as the audible shot rang out beyond the door. The pistol's discharges rattled the door's hinges, and as the bullets passed through the wood, splinters and the mist of blood polluted the air about him. The scent of wood and the metallic taste of blood assaulted his senses.

Time seemed to speed up again as Will and his brother were hurled to the floor, immobilized from the percussion. Will's senses were reeling, his vision blurry, and his hearing muffled as he watched the distorted figure that was Richard writhing on the floor beside him, his faint speech barely audible.

Richard turned over, grasping at his hip. His pants were saturated with blood that was now starting to puddle on the floor. The pain was a blunt throbbing agony. He grasped it and squeezed it as if his efforts would stay the pain. He could see it was merely a flesh wound; the bullet had passed through. "Will," he said as he turned his attention to his brother, who was almost senseless.

Will was looking about the room as though he were trying to regain his eyesight. At the mention of his name, he looked at Richard with some discomfort as if his eyes weren't focusing. Splinters projected from his temple, and blood ran down his cheek and neck in tiny rivulets, trickling to the floor.

"Can you hear me, Will? Can you see me?" His questions were asked with panic as he heard Lucy's footfalls on the front porch.

"I'm good, Richard. I'm good… I just need a minute."

He could tell Will's senses were reeling out of control; the two shots that penetrated the door had left him seemingly concussed. The footfalls moved toward one of the windows, and Lucy's silhouette peered through briefly before they resumed toward the door.

Richard was frantic as he started to pull himself up, and fear and rage coursed through him, numbing the pain of his gunshot. A cold sensation came over him, and a chill filled the air. His breath was now visible, and he paused, now on his knees. Before him stood the woman from his room, only she wasn't the spectre he remembered. Ophelia was not the drowning, gasping spectre he had seen before, but a beautiful woman with warm features despite the gelid aura that encompassed her. She was reaching out, grasping his wrists and pulling him to his feet, forcing him to stand as the front door swung open.

Lucy entered, her revolver held before her gaze roved to Will then to him. She glanced at the wound on his hip, and a delight came over her, noticing she hadn't missed after all.

"Any smart words, Mr. Stilton?" she asked as she trained the pistol to his chest. As she cocked back the hammer, that horrid *click, clack* of death, the room abruptly fell cold. The icy chill enveloped everything, like a frost that seemed to be pulled from the walls only to be overwhelmed by the ectoplasm that oozed from the ceiling, that poured from the cracks and crevices of the walls and floorboards.

Lucy looked about, horrified. Clearly, she had never before witnessed such paranormal activity. Long threads of the ectoplasmic substance dripped from the ceiling in long thin strands as the atmosphere in the abode became more frigid.

"I am done with you, Mr. Stilton," she announced, turning her attention back to Richard.

Richard's vision flew to Will, who was starting to get to his knees, gawking at the paranormal phenomena about them. Richard stepped forward to grasp the gun, but Lucy pulled the trigger, and he froze for a second as if bracing himself in anticipation of a discharge, of a bullet about to penetrate his chest, but it was not to come. Instead, there was Lucy, squeezing the trigger with all of her might, the hammer refusing to fall. Will was now on his feet, standing with Richard, and they watched on in horror as she glared at the two. Lucy's eyes were wide, her mouth agape as if trying desperately to draw air. She dropped the pistol and clutched at her throat, at the handprints that appeared about her trachea. She gasped and gargled as water started to pour from the corners of her mouth. Her head wrenched backward as if someone were pulling her hair. Her body convulsed, and her chest heaved desperately. Suddenly she was dropped to the floor, gasping for her life and grasping at Richard's leg.

"H... help... m... me!" she begged. Her body was suddenly hurled to the wall, pinned as though a weight were forced upon her. Lucy shook her head in torturous pain, trying to scream in anguish, but only a whisper emerged as she was hurled to the floor like a worn, ragged doll, grotesquely gargling and choking, dragged down the hall into the darkness. Richard watched with his brother, stricken at the ferocity of the attack, at the anger and horror in her eyes as she clawed at the floor, water pouring from her mouth, leaving a broken, splattered trail. Richard grabbed his brother's wrist and pulled him out the door. The two fled the cabin and the silent cries that resonated from within.

Will's fingertips fluttered over his face at the splinters that extended from his face and neck. He winced in pain as he fingered the ones that were easiest to grasp, pulling them out. A sharp pain overcame him, followed by a sense of relief.

"We get inside, grab our shit, and get out of here," uttered Richard as he looked at his hip.

"Does it hurt?" asked Will.

Richard shook his head. "It feels like a blunt pain. It's going numb."

"Shit, you're going into shock."

"That's shocking!" Richard laughed slightly as the two pushed their way through the door and started making their way up the stairs. Will sighed. Even now, the guy is in a jovial mood, or at least so out of it that his body's state of shock is "happy." Richard was walking just fine, and he hadn't lost much blood. The wound was superficial, but he still needed to get to a hospital.

"May I be the first to protest against your departure, Messrs. Stilton?" The familiar voice of Mrs. Law greeted them as she came down the hallway, her pistol trained on them. She paused to observe the wound on Richard's hip and the splinters in Will's face and neck. "Not the ideal sharpshooter with a pistol, is she? Allow me to reassure you; I am a far better shot than my Lucy counterpart."

Will and Richard said nothing.

"I truly hope you haven't dispatched with her. I will be terribly put out if that is the case. Either way, your stay here at the Law estates has come to its end, and I wish to see you on your way. Your van has been nicely packed with all of your equipment and any other effects you may have brought with you. Save those documents that shan't leave these grounds. I believe you know of which I speak, Messrs. Stilton."

"The letters and photographs," stated Will, his eyes filled with a hatred even Mrs. Law could not match.

She nodded. "Among other papers. Now, if you will be so kind as to turn about and proceed down the stairs." She gestured with her pistol.

Will could see the revolver was heavy in her hands but not near the burden it bore Lucy. In fact, she seemed quite comfortable with the pistol in her grip, as though it were, in fact, an extension of her arm.

CHAPTER THIRTEEN

HAUNTED

Will proceeded down the stairs, just behind Richard, into the foyer and through a locked door that, to the naked and untrained eye, would not have existed. The corridor beyond was dank and dark. Sconces lit the hall, and the doors that lined it were nothing more than partition shadows, eerie in their symmetry.

"Parts of this mansion are far older than I," she uttered as if the duo before her were interested. She continued, "The ghosts in this place are very real, Messrs. Stilton. I have seen them, called to them, screamed at them, and I have missed them dearly."

They halted in front of a door as she fumbled the keys and opened it. With the flick of a light switch, an old library came alight with thousands of volumes of books and papers adorning shelves of two levels. Their spines were extended, revealing their names, their titles as if yearning to be opened and their secrets revealed. The air was musty with the scent of old pages in decay, of faltering bindings, rotting off the shelf. A dampness permeated. The kind that only relishes the darkness and is the blight of books, which brings a degeneration fueled by time.

"My husband's old library, his original study." Mrs. Law spoke as though the past was choking her, drawing her tears to their surface, as if the pain of loss was still so very real.

She directed Will and Richard to a small staircase at the back of the room, and the three ventured to the second level and to a desk, seemingly as ancient as the library itself but in immaculate condition. Its surface was polished and tidy, and a handful of books lay open.

"This is where I spend most of my free time, Messrs. Stilton. This is where I see my Edgar most, shut from the world as I was shut from his life." She opened a cabinet to reveal a number of casks, four of which were tapped. "My private stock of wine," she said, turning with a smile and a hint of pride as she drew a bottle, poured herself a glass of wine, and gently placed it back.

"I loved my husband very much, Mr. Stilton," she said to Will, cradling the glass close to her chest. "Doting on him maybe a little too much. But alas, he loved Ophelia more. Such is the way of life, Mr. Stilton, love and loss walking hand in hand, but I cannot forgive my late husband for his actions. Do you know what it's like, Mr. Stilton, to watch your beloved fall into the arms of another?"

Will stood silently, expressionless with his brother.

"I'll tell you, it's horrible. At first, they tried to keep it a secret, their affair. They even hid her pregnancy for a time, but time itself cannot be trusted, and it, too, reveals all things.

"Thankfully, I was already privy to their goings-on. Lucy had already proven her loyalty to me, and, through her, I knew most of what transpired between my sweet Edgar and his new precious Ophelia." She said the names with such disgust, and her face twisted as the words spilled out as though they were a vile taste lingering on her tongue. "I could not bear to sit by and watch the treacherous plans they concocted come to fruition, Mr. Stilton."

Now she looked at Will with fury in her eyes. "I simply could not. He was my husband, not hers. I may have married into this family, into this wealth, Mr. Stilton, but Ophelia was nothing more than a harlot."

As stoic as she was, Will noticed the pistol starting to quiver ever so slightly, whether from the weight or the emotion.

"We tried to have children twice, but they were both stillborn."

He could see the emotion welling up in her eyes, a redness, the glint of accumulating tears that started to tumble down her cheeks. "Saraphima grew, as did my resentment for her. She was a constant reminder of my failure, Mr. Stilton. What I could not give and what I could not have."

Finally, Will spoke. "Why are you telling us all of this?"

She regarded him as she might an inquisitive child, almost pleased he asked. "Closure, Mr. Stilton, closure! I don't need you skulking around here like the other restless spirits."

A certain boldness grew in Will. He wanted to draw more information from her without being direct. "So you killed them," he stated, as a matter of fact.

She scoffed. "Oh heavens, no, my dear Mr. Stilton. Murder is so unbecoming for a lady of my stature. I have my Lucy to thank. She really does have my best interests at heart, you know." She walked over to a cabinet and drew from it a bottle of wine, poured a glass, and set it before Will on a small serving table. "No, Mr. Stilton, you will be joining my late husband and his daughter, you and your brother." She gestured to Richard as she poured him a glass also. "Quietly hidden away in your own cask in my private stock of wine."

Now Will knew, his heart sank, and his throat tightened ever so slightly. "But the gravestones…"

Mrs. Law waved them off with a modicum of irritation. "Merely politics, Mr. Stilton. Edgar still has family, and with family come questions, questions I am not willing to answer. So, after his lover, Ophelia,"—she said the name with the same vile taste on her tongue—"Accidentally 'fell,' striking her head on the fountain and drowning, my Edgar became increasingly depressed and suspicious of me." She sighed, running her fingers along the brim of her glass of wine.

"But he was bound to his daughter, the one that I didn't give him, that I couldn't accept. For thirty-four years, I watched those two, watched as I faded away, as I became the ghost that stalked the halls and corridors of this place, lonely and yearning for the love of a husband who was still here but not for me." The emotion poured out as she spoke. Wiping the developing tears from her eyes, she realized she was losing her composure. "Apologies, Messrs. Stilton."

"No worries," Richard chimed in with a smirk, seemingly almost amused at her anguish.

"Anyhow, Messrs. Stilton, once the police found my late husband's car crashed and abandoned miles away from anywhere at the bottom of a cliff with no bodies in it, and the search party found no trace of them in the forests surrounding, they could only conclude that the fauna had carried them off. And I, ever the clever one, called in a missing persons report, demonstrating my concern." She sipped her wine and took the briefest moment to savour it. "Do you recall our conversation regarding skeletons, Mr. Stilton?" She was looking hard at Will. "The skeletons we keep can haunt us to the grave. A fortunate few can utterly ignore their bony features glaring back at them from the darkest recesses of their minds." A glimmer of a smile crept on her lips. "And there are people such as myself, Messrs Stilton. I collect skeletons. They hold a particular leverage: the ability to destroy marriages, shred families, expose scandals, and ruin careers." Mrs. Law leaned on her desk, taking on a strong authoritarian posture. "I own a plethora of skeletons, Messrs. Stilton. I make it my business to know what secrets the people of Brackenstone store in their pathetic closets." She waved her hand in the air as though what she was about to divulge was trivial at best. "Affairs, scandals, addictions; some I contribute to so they may continue to indulge. In short, I own them—our local judge, the police commissioner and some of his detectives, the head of our little bank, the lawyers to my late husband's will. I even own the damned baker and his wife. In short, Messrs. Stilton, I own this town. I get what I want, and the consequences of what I could wreak on their wretched lives are far greater than if they choose not to comply with my wishes."

She took a sip of her wine, meeting Will's gaze. "That was some time ago, and lately, my workers are reporting more and more ghostly apparitions haunting these grounds, scaring them from their work as though they were omens of doom. Those who recognized my husband and Saraphima are all gone now, run off over the nights in their fright."

Will sat forward. "And the extra body in the tomb? Hidden like a dirty secret?" he said as he reached for the wine. Its bouquet was strong as he brought it to his nose, trying to suppress his fear.

"Alice, Mr. Stilton, was nothing more than a thorn. She had no bearing on the affairs between my late Edgar and his daughter. No, she was merely a mistake, a small blunder on my part that had to be dealt with in the most drastic of measures."

Will sipped the wine and felt his face register pleasure. It was not like anything he had ever tasted before. Observing him, Mrs. Law grinned slightly with clear pride.

"And so you ran her down with your Delta," Richard blurted. "We've seen the car."

She regarded Richard for a minute, pausing in thought, and Will got the impression she was enjoying this.

"Have you ever watched someone go mad, Messrs. Stilton? Have you witnessed an individual fall from whatever grace they possessed to be reduced to a bumbling, ranting, wailing wretch of their former self?" Her eyes jumped from Will to Richard, then back to Will, who just looked on. He had no response with which to interrupt, but in his mind, he recalled the night with Richard.

"I watched from afar as she meandered about the estate, conversing with no one but herself, gesturing to things that weren't there and over time, hurling items at something or someone only she could see, all the while screaming angrily." She sighed and for a moment, and Will thought he could see a hint of regret in her eyes.

"Alice would speak of a male presence that would visit her at night time and would sometimes follow her about the estate." She looked Will in the eyes hard. "A man whose head would fall off when she looked at him. There are no more men in this mansion anymore, save you and your brother. The only other men on this estate are those that work out in the orchards and vineyards. The funny part of it is, I had my Edgar beheaded with an axe, Messrs. Stilton. Now there is a bit of horror in that."

She chuckled to herself, then turned serious again. "Sirs, occasionally, when someone of my standing has much to lose, they have very few options. So when I send my Lucy into town to run errands, and she comes back bloody, with her car damaged and a story that Alice, a young woman in my employ, simply ran from the forest and threw herself in front of the vehicle, killed by a fellow employee, what stories and attention would start to grow and fester?"

Will took another small sip of the wine. He couldn't place the taste; it was so unfamiliar, but it did take his edge off a little bit, calming him down ever so slightly yet still keeping himself sharp. "Or you could just own it and admit that you ran the poor girl down with the car and hid her body."

She scoffed at the notion. "I must confess, you and your brother are not complete invalids. You did manage to find this little piece for me." She held up the bequest left for Saraphima. "Little good it was; I was not unaware of his plans and used my vast leverage with the law firm to have the will drafted in my favour when Edgar had finished his little ploy. Perhaps it was foolish of me to allow him to think himself clever."

For a moment, she looked as though she were drawing on some distant memory. "It matters not anymore. His draft for his precious daughter has long since been incinerated, which will be the fate of all here." She gestured to the bequest and the plethora of pictures and letters on her desk. "Then there will be no trace of my Edgar or his daughter on my grounds. After seeing your credentials, I was hopeful that with your degree of scepticism and investigative tactics, you would be the one to debunk the ideology of ghosts at the Law estate.

"Clearly, I was mistaken, and now I find I must dispatch the pair of you before you are my undoing. I do not consider myself a murderer, Messrs. Stilton. I am a survivor who will go to any lengths." She smiled, taking another sip of her wine, relishing the taste, then sniffed its aromatic bouquet and gestured to Richard's glass. "You really should try it, Mr. Stilton, it is quite robust. This is the closest I get to my Edgar anymore."

She looked at Will with a sinister smile. "And that is the closest you will ever be to your Saraphima."

The colour drained from Will's face, and a consternation of dread befell him as he dropped the glass on the floor. For the first time, Mrs. Law laughed. She howled in most sinister mirth as she relished Will's reaction, the gun firmly trained on the two.

"I give you credit, sirs. You are good at what you do, and now you will be that which you have hunted for so long. Perhaps someone will hunt you with equal fervour as you have hunted." With that, the revolver discharged, its blast reverberating off the book-lined walls, and the room shook. A spray of red mist filled the air, painting the railing behind Will with its gore.

Richard turned to see his brother freeze for a moment then look down at the red spot that appeared on his abdomen. A shudder rocked his body, and he met Richard's eye with a grimace as he seemed to realize he had been shot. Mrs. Law's laughter echoed as Richard, crying out, rushed to Will's aid, who was now slumping in his chair, clutching at his wound.

"This is where you die, Mr. Stilton," she exclaimed as she directed the pistol to Richard, cocking the hammer back.

It was as if all the blood had drained from Richard. His body was cold, his hair stood on end, and he felt an electric force envelope him as he was abruptly thrown across the room when the revolver discharged again. The bullet struck the railing where Richard was standing, spraying shards of wood into the air and littering the floor below.

A look of shock and bewilderment formed on Mrs. Law's face, followed by anger as she scowled at the air. "No! They are mine!" She fired again and again, but she missed as Richard was dragged across the floor by some unseen force, the bullets failing to find their mark.

"I will have one of them!" she bellowed in rage as she turned her attention back to Will, cocking the hammer once again only to falter as if some invisible force had stayed her hand. The space around her became electric, and suddenly she was hurled to the wall. The casks of wine rocked about as she struggled with the unseen force that had her pinned, and then she was thrown to the floor.

Richard's heart was racing as he attacked, yelling with rage as he was upon her, clasping at her hand with the pistol. All of her regal composure was now lost as she screamed, clawed, and struck Richard, trying to prevent him from prying the gun from her grasp. Her nails dug into his cheeks and neck as she clawed at his chest and arms, but he was fueled by the bitter resentment for her and a frenzy for the survival of Will.

He tossed the pistol over the railing, and, picking up Mrs. Law, he brought her down upon her desk. It cracked and groaned under the force. Wine glasses and decanters shattered. She howled in a painful outburst as shards of glass embedded themselves in her back. Richard left her writhing in her agony and quickly scooped up his brother.

Will groaned as Richard hoisted him over his massive shoulders. "Easy now, I'm not dead yet!" he uttered.

"And you won't die, Will. You won't die," he replied, though he could feel the warmth of his brother's blood spilling onto his back as he hustled down the stairs toward the door. Behind him, he could hear Mrs. Law's curses and profanities as she hoisted herself from her desk, bits of glass projecting from her torso. She yelled threats and promises of ill demise as she gave chase down the stairs.

Nearly at the bottom, Richard looked back to see the twisted, mangled shell of Mrs. Law clawing her way down the stairs. Blood and obscenities poured from her as she moved like something inhuman, not the regal Mrs. Law they had met, but the mind and the soul driven by madness and obsession.

Richard tore across the room with Will as his burden, but Mrs. Law reached the floor and bolted toward them, biting Will's shoulder and pulling him from Richard's back. Will cried out as he fought against her, now atop of him, clawing and striking violently. He favoured his abdomen as he fought and defended himself from her onslaught. He, at last, managed to land a solid blow to her jaw.

Mrs. Law reeled back, and Richard pounced on her, dragging her from his brother, only to have her turn on him. She dug her fingers into the side of his neck and tried to bite his throat. He pushed her back, her jaws snapping and clamping like some wild beast. Pulling her from him, he tried to throw her again, but she refused to let go. Biting down on his arm, she held on with everything she had. Richard cried out, trying to pry her from him, her teeth slowly sinking deeper.

Amidst the scuffling, Will pulled himself to one knee. The pistol lay at the far end of the room. As he struggled, a hand appeared, and Will looked up to Edgar Law. He was tall and strong with broad shoulders and large hands. What features were distinguishable were hard yet gentle, and he grasped Will's hand and hoisted him to his feet and then he was gone. Will found himself holding an axe. He did not hesitate; he rushed over and brought the axe down upon Mrs. Law.

She wailed as the blade struck her in the back, severing her spine, her body falling limp. Will stood back, poised for another blow as she fell to the floor, her eyes void of the malice they just bore, and her features weren't so twisted. A calm enveloped the room as everything fell silent, but the atmosphere was still heavy and foreboding.

Will threw the axe to the floor, far from her reach and stumbled to Richard, who caught him up. Richard, whose neck and arms were strewn with claw marks and bites and whose hip displayed a gunshot, bore his brother's weight with every ounce of strength he could seemingly muster. He closed the door behind them, sealing Mrs. Law in the library.

Eleanor Law lay twitching in her torment. Her breathing was laboured with shallow, whimpering sobs of mumbled apologies as her eyes, wide with terror, glared. Standing over her was a pretty woman with short brown curly locks and a kerchief, wearing overalls with dirt stains on the knees. Saraphima smiled as she stood over Mrs. Law. In her small earth-covered hands was the axe.

Richard pushed his way out the front door and gingerly placed Will in the van.

"I could go for a scotch right about now," Will uttered.

"You just hold on, Will. Just hold on," retorted Richard in a comforting voice.

Looking in the back of the van, Will saw that it was neatly packed with all of the equipment they had come with, or so it appeared.

Will looked out the window toward Saraphima's cabin as they pulled out of the drive toward the road. They watched the tall trees, bent over the road, pass by as they drove off. They were finally leaving that forsaken place. Will turned to his brother. "I'm feeling cold, Richard." Then everything went black.

Time had dragged by. Richard was sitting in the waiting room of the hospital when his phone rang. It was Stacey.

"Hey, I'm just checking in to see if there are any updates?"

"No updates yet, Stacey, but thanks for checking on us."

There was a sigh on the other end. "How long has it been now?"

"Almost two days. The doctors say he's actually pretty good. He should have lost more blood than he did. It's almost as though something was keeping him from bleeding out…"

"How strange," she replied. "And how are you holding up, hun?"

Richard touched the bandages on his hip and looked at the plethora of coverings on his arms and neck. "I'm doing good, sweetie. A little stiff, but I'm good."

"What about the police?"

"What about them?" he chuckled to himself. "They went to the Law estate only to find one rusted pistol and no bodies. I get the sense they don't even want to go back. It's as if something chased them away from there. I tell you, this whole town is superstitious when it comes to that place."

"Hmm, probably for good reason. Okay, hun, I'll call you later and see how you two are doing. Everyone here is fine. We're all looking forward to having you two back."

"Thanks, sweetie." Richard hung up the phone and sat down, choking back tears. He hated this. It was eating him up.

"Don't worry, Mr. Stilton," came a fair feminine voice. Richard turned to find a short, pretty woman sitting beside him. Her hair was in beautiful brown locks that came to her chin. She wore a pretty sundress that accentuated her bust. Her smile was adorable, and her eyes were enchanting. Richard's blood ran cold as he beheld her. "You're the garden girl!" he nearly stammered.

"Saraphima is my name, Mr. Stilton, and you can address me as such." She smiled a nearly seductive, cocky smile. "Your worry is all for not. Mr. William will be just fine."

Richard was taken aback, speechless, as he looked on. "And you're welcome, for stopping the bleeding, that is. For a big strong guy, you sure moved slow enough! But you're not built for speed, are you?" She smiled again and rose from her seat. "I've already spoken with Mr. William, and I will now bid you fare-thee-well. You're a good brother Mr. Stilton." She pushed on his cheek with a hand that was cold yet soft.

Richard looked back, but she was gone, and moments later, doctors came forth.

It had nearly been a week since Will was released, and he and Richard had returned home. He was content and relieved to be among his comforts and familiarities, from the atmosphere to the aromas of a home. Richard checked in on him now and again, and he too expressed his delight to be back at the sanctuary that was his abode. The scratches were nearly healed, and though the gunshot caused more trauma, the knife wound in his side hurt far more, but it was healing very well. The doctors said that Will's abdomen would make a full recovery, but the trauma from the bullet left a hole and surrounding trauma in his liver. His right kidney was bruised, as was the diaphragm under his right lung, which made breathing painful at times. Will hadn't touched a bottle since he'd been home. Instead, he was content to imbibe coffees and teas, wrapped in a blanket on his sofa or in his wing-backed chair. He exuded an air of reminiscence, recalling some grand memory. Once in a while, he'd indulge in a nice pint of stout, doing whatever he pleased. He hadn't sworn off the hard liquor. He hadn't felt like it was needed or wanted in the opportune moment, nor was he under any stress. Oddly enough, letting go of Saraphima felt very much like letting go of Brynn. The emotions were not too dissimilar, but the circumstances between the two made coming to terms with the gardener woman with the wide smile, brown hair, and dirty overalls somewhat easier, though he found himself missing her company at times. He would catch himself looking out his windows at his own garden, secretly hoping to see her smiling back, but to no avail.

Everyone back at the institute was happy to see the duo return. Will was in good spirits, which were amplified with the presentation of a bottle of scotch. He relished "opportune moments" and wasted no time in pouring himself and his brother a generous glass. Richard was delighted to receive a new refurbished laptop that lit up like something otherworldly.

Time had passed, and wounds had healed, for the most part. Will knew his physical scars would taunt him now and again, but an emotional and spiritual wound remained. Saraphima would forever haunt his thoughts and his feelings. He, in a sense, was now haunted.

Will readied himself for bed. He was eager for some time off, then back to the institute. He pulled the covers over his shoulders and snuggled into the pillow. As he drifted, he felt the sensation of an arm about him, drawing him in, breasts pressing against his back, and a soft, cool kiss on his shoulder.

About the Author

Poet and storyteller Rene M. Gerrits takes his fascination for the paranormal and supernatural to a whole new level, creating investigators and brothers Will and Richard of Stilton Paranormal Research Institute in their complex and witty dynamic. His enthusiasm for all things that defy explanation started in his youth and has not wavered to this day, as he combines his talent and his intrigue to create a world where the supernatural and the living are intertwined with the brothers at the center.

Published as a poet specializing in the fantastical and the macabre, he now brings a novel that combines his talent and his intrigue to create a world where the supernatural and the living are interwoven.

CPSIA information can be obtained
at www.ICGtesting.com
Printed in the USA
LVHW090916201221
706582LV00018B/146